THE
BEAUTIFUL
GAME

THE BEAUTIFUL GAME

DAVID SKUY

JAMES LORIMER & COMPANY LTD., PUBLISHERS
TORONTO

James Lorimer & Company Ltd., Publishers acknowledges the support of the
Ontario Arts Council. We acknowledge the support of the Canada Council
for the Arts which last year invested $24.3 million in writing and publishing
throughout Canada. We acknowledge the Government of Ontario through the
Ontario Media Development Corporation's Ontario Book Initiative.

Cover design: Meredith Bangay
Cover image: Shutterstock

Library and Archives Canada Cataloguing in Publication

Skuy, David, 1963-, author
    The beautiful game / David Skuy.

Issued in print and electronic formats.
ISBN 978-1-4594-0962-0 (paperback).--ISBN 978-1-4594-0964-4 (epub)
    I. Title.

PS8637.K72B43 2015   jC813'.6   C2015-903880-4
C2015-903881-2

James Lorimer &
Company Ltd., Publishers
317 Adelaide Street West,
Suite 1002
Toronto, ON, Canada
M5V 1P9
www.lorimer.ca

Canadian edition
(978-1-4594-0962-0)
distributed by:
Formac Lorimer Books
5502 Atlantic Street
Halifax, NS, Canada
B3H 1G4

American edition
(978-1-4594-0963-7)
distributed by:
Lerner Publishing Group
1251 Washington Ave N
Minneapolis, MN, USA
55401

Printed and bound in Canada.
Manufactured by Friesens Corporation in Altona, Manitoba, Canada in August 2015
Job #215802

Here's to the Watford gang for keeping
The Beautiful Game alive in my heart.

Cody Dorsett kicked at the grass with his cleats and tried to catch his breath. Coach Trevor had been on the warpath all practice. He'd really stepped things up lately. The Lions only had eleven players on the roster, so fitness was a big deal. While they grumbled about the hard work sometimes, Cody knew deep down everyone loved it.

"Okay, this is a six-on-five drill. Attacking side has to get a shot on goal — or they run the length of the field and back. The last guy does ten push-ups," Trevor yelled between cupped hands. "Work the ball around — and no mistakes."

A tall, lanky kid, with wavy blond hair, sidestepped over to Cody. "We win six in a row and Trevor gets cranky?" he said.

Bone-tired, Cody still had to laugh. Kenneth was forever cracking jokes, although when it came to soccer he was deadly serious. He was probably the Lions' best midfielder.

"Support the ball this time," Trevor called out. "Quick short passes, and strike when you see an opening. You're using the long ball too much. Keep possession."

Kenneth pushed forward. "I hate defenders — they're so defender-y. And they smell like . . . defence. It's close, but I think Luca smells the worst." Kenneth pointed to a short, powerfully built kid with straight black hair.

"I smell a shot wide right — enjoy the run, attackers," Luca said. He and William, another defender, high-fived.

"Don't know why we even have defenders on the team. All they do is keep the ball out of the net — like you're gonna win a game that way," Kenneth said.

Kenneth held his hand down low to Cody. He hesitated, then gave Kenneth's hand a light slap. The midfielder ran off toward Paulo, who had the ball just in from the right sideline, about thirty-five metres from goal. Paulo had only been with the team for a month and he was totally one of the boys. Cody still felt like an outsider. He was obviously on the team, but not good friends with anyone — not really. Cody wondered whether he'd ever fit in the way Paulo did already.

He knew why he didn't, of course. All the guys knew. Cody had told them last month after a tournament. How it had started with the pain in the back of his right leg, and how Dr. Charya told him he had a tumour and she'd have to operate. About his hair falling out, the dizziness, and the chemotherapy. The chemicals had killed the cancer in his body — but the cancer was still part of him.

Always would be. He'd always be the kid with cancer. He knew the guys found it creepy. He couldn't blame them, either. He'd had something gross growing in his body. He found it creepy, too.

Cody watched Paulo feed the ball down the sideline to Brandon. Brandon pressed forward and shovelled a pass to Kenneth, who made as if to continue that way and then spun back and carried it cross field. Paulo hustled in on the overlap and Kenneth rolled it to him. Cody cut inside. Jordan, the other striker, did the same.

"Spacing, boys," Trevor bellowed. "I don't want two players in the same spot. Cody and Jordan, spread out. Give him someone to pass to."

Cody flushed and backpedalled to the outside. Austin, the outside right back defender, moved up to mark him.

Stupid mistake. He'd seen Jordan. Probably should have said something. He didn't like telling the guys what to do. Kenneth, Paulo, or Luca were the guys who did that.

Paulo slowly dragged the ball along with his right foot. Kenneth called for it. Brandon made a short run to the box. Ryan, another midfielder, took off to the other sideline. Paulo caught Cody's eye, only for a brief second, and that was enough.

Cody spun around Austin's right shoulder. He heard the thud of the ball. Paulo had delivered. He could only hope he wasn't offside. The ball curled over Austin's desperate leap. Cody reached out with his left foot to control it.

No whistle: onside!

The ball bounced inside a little more than he wanted it to, giving William a chance to cut him off.

David spread his arms wide and came out to take away the angle. The super-athletic goalie was always tough to beat, even in practice. With William half a step away, Cody struck the ball with his right foot, aiming short side. David reached out his right hand — too late.

"Yeah, baby," Kenneth whooped from behind.

The ball ticked the post — wide left.

"Yeah, baby — I predict pain in your future," Luca said gleefully.

"You're a monster," Kenneth said to Luca.

Luca's face fell. "I have a sensitive side, you know." He paused. "Okay, I don't, really. Enjoy the run."

Kenneth growled at Luca and ran off downfield. Cody threw his head back and stared up at the sky. Two inches the other way and the ball would have been in. Brutal.

"Good effort," Trevor said. "The chance was there. I don't mind that."

The kind words cheered him a little. Trevor was tough to please. Cody lengthened his stride. May as well get this drill over with. His right leg usually felt tight after a hard kick. Recently, the last week or so, he hadn't felt any stiffness. That had to be good?

"Yo, speed demon. Slow down," Kenneth said to him.

Cody was passing them all.

"Sorry," he said. He cleared his throat and matched Kenneth's stride. "Dumb kick. I messed up the pass and had to hurry."

"You hit the freakin' post," Kenneth said. "I don't think you messed up too bad. Bad luck. Besides, the smell of those defenders was getting to me."

Cody wished he could be more like Kenneth. He could never think of a comeback fast enough, and by the time he did the moment was gone.

"Whenever you're even with a guy like that on the back line I'm gonna chip it over his head," Paulo said. "No one in this league has your speed."

Paulo was always going on like that. Cody knew it wasn't really true. Tons of guys were fast.

Jordan, Brandon, and Ryan had gone ahead early and were almost done. Cody decided to hang back. He'd missed the shot. He should come last and do the push-ups.

"Awesome Idea Alert," Kenneth said suddenly. They were about twenty-five metres away. "If all three of us cross the line at the same time, no one is last, and no one has to do push-ups."

"That's good teamwork," Paulo laughed. "I'm in."

"I missed," Cody said. "I'll be last."

Kenneth shook his head. "Do what you're told. You're not old enough to make your own decisions."

"He's practically a baby," Paulo said.

"I can . . . I'm not . . ."

"We're sorta joking here, Cody," Kenneth grinned.

Cody hated himself sometimes. He was always making a fool of himself like that.

"I . . . umm . . . I know . . . Let's all finish together," he managed.

Kenneth threw his arms across their shoulders about ten metres from the goal. "*We don't stop for nobody. We don't stop for nobody*," he chanted.

Paulo joined in.

"Someone please stop them," Luca begged.

They crossed the goal line and Kenneth threw his arms in the air. "Aww. Sorry, Coach Trevor. No one finished last — so I guess no push-ups. Maybe next time."

Trevor rubbed the side of his face with his hand. "Or . . . We could say you all came last?"

"We could," Kenneth said, "but then you'd make me cry and . . . no one wants to see that."

"I do. I do," Luca said.

"You really are a monster," Kenneth said.

"A monster with a sensitive side," Luca corrected him.

Trevor pointed to the ground and flicked his eyebrows.

Kenneth dropped to his knees and held his hands to the sky. "Cruel world!" he yelled. He began to pound out the push-ups. "One, two, three, four . . . "

Paulo counted with him, and then Luca did too — and then everyone. Cody counted to himself.

"Bring it in, lads," Trevor said. "I think we'll shut it down. We have a game tomorrow against the Storm and I don't want you tired out."

"I feel so lucky," Kenneth said to Cody.

"Tough practice," Cody said.

He really was a total goof. He should've said "I hate it when we don't run in practice" or "Trevor's such a wimp." Pathetic.

"I'm thinking we need a new coach," Luca said, coming over. "He's lost his edge."

"The guy is clueless about soccer," Kenneth said. "All he did was play pro for ten years in Europe and the US."

Cody was about to mention that Paulo's dad, the assistant coach, also played pro.

Luca beat him to the punch. "What about Paulo's dad, Leandro?" he said. "Freakin' loser played pro in Brazil for something like twelve years. What do Brazilians know about soccer?"

The guys sat on the ground around Trevor in a semi-circle.

"Let's talk a bit about our next game," Trevor said.

"I could spend the rest of my life not talking about the Storm," David said.

"Maybe aliens kidnapped Timothy and he won't play," Luca said.

"Maybe they'll do painful experiments on him and discover why he's such a jerk," Paulo said.

"Okay, lads," Trevor said. "I know many of you have good reasons to dislike some of the guys on the Storm. We need to keep calm and play our game. They're going to be chirping at you — expect it. The best revenge is to win."

"We beat them in the tournament. We'll beat them again," Paulo said.

"You've heard me say it before. Timothy and his crew did us a favour when they quit our team," Trevor said. "Timothy can play, and so can Antonio, Michael, and Tyler, but . . . "

"You left out John, Coach," Kenneth grinned.

"Let's not be mean," Trevor said, but Cody could see he was smiling.

Cody clenched his fists. Timothy and his crew had come up with some choice nicknames for him when they used to play with the Lions: Egg-Head, Eggy, Cue Ball, Humpty Dumpty — as if he wanted his hair to fall out! A rush of emotion surged through him.

"We'll win because we want it more," Cody said, eyes burning.

They all looked at him.

He forced a grin. Inside, he was mortified. He was always saying awkward things.

Paulo came to his rescue. "Cody's right," he said. "We worry too much about them."

"The Lions don't need to worry 'bout nothing! Let the Storm worry about us!" Kenneth said.

The boys let out a roar.

Trevor nodded slowly. "I'm liking that idea — very much. Great practice today, too — focused, hard-working. You're a team, and together you're a force to be reckoned with." He looked to the sidelines. A few of the parents had come onto the field. "I think your parents are getting restless. Sorry for the early practice on a Saturday. I know thirteen-year-old boys enjoy their sleep. It's tough to get practice time. There just aren't enough fields."

"I heard the city is building a new community centre," William said, "and it's gonna have four soccer fields."

"Yeah. My mom told me that, too," Brandon said.

"There's a company building a factory, and in return for a building permit they've agreed to give the city money for the community centre. It's also going to have a pool, a gym, and a library," Trevor said. "Won't be ready for a few years, but it's still great news."

"Awesome," Luca said. "Kenneth could totally use more gym time."

Kenneth flexed his arms. "It would be nice to turn these spaghetti arms into Popsicle sticks."

Luca put an arm around his shoulders. "Bro, that's crazed. Let's shoot for thick string or maybe pipe cleaners."

"The city is holding a rally at City Hall Square this afternoon," Trevor said. "I understand there's free food and music and . . . sounds like a good time."

Kenneth gasped. "Coach, I gotta go. All my life I dreamed of stuffing my face with free food at City Hall — this afternoon."

"I gotta go, too, Coach," Luca said. "I've always dreamed of stuffing my face while I watch Kenneth stuffing his face . . . at City Hall this afternoon."

Trevor waved his hand in the air. "Game time tomorrow is ten thirty. Get there an hour early, please, so we can warm up properly. And again, good practice. You all put in a great effort."

"And more importantly, let's meet at twelve o'clock at City Hall Square," Kenneth said. "I'll be the guy with five hot dogs in his hands."

"I'll be the guy taking five hot dogs from Kenneth," Luca said.

Cody tried to think of something to add.

"Get going already, then," Trevor said, laughing. He headed to the sidelines where the parents were milling about.

Cody got up. Missed his chance.

"Paulo, you in?" Kenneth said.

"Like I'm not gonna eat five hot dogs — and french fries and pizza if they have them?" Paulo said.

"William?" Luca said.

"I'm there," he said. "My dad's all over this factory thing. My whole family's going."

"My mom's part of it, too," Brandon said, "so I'll be there."

Cody wanted to go. He couldn't just show up uninvited — he'd look totally lame. Kenneth and Luca were best friends. Paulo was always included — everyone liked him. Lost in those thoughts Cody wandered to the sidelines. Kenneth ran up beside him.

"So you want me to swing by your place or should we meet at the Square?" he said.

Cody was too startled to reply.

"What do you wanna do?" Kenneth said.

"Umm . . . don't know, I'll . . . "

"Easy enough for us to come over. We can bike," Kenneth said. "See you later — and next time hit the net."

"Sorry about that," Cody said.

Kenneth tilted his head.

"Joking, right?" Cody said.

Kenneth flashed a thumbs-up. "You'll figure me out eventually. Basically, everything I say is stupid."

"I'll try and remember," Cody said. "See ya later."

His mom was waving at him from the sidelines. He turned away. He could feel his face getting all hot, which meant he was blushing. Kenneth was usually good about including him in stuff. Probably felt bad for him. They'd been extra nice since he told them about his cancer.

When would things be normal?

Probably never.

Cody heaved a sigh.

"I told you it's just for an hour," Cody said. "I'm meeting Kenneth and the guys at City Hall Square. There's free food and stuff. Practice wasn't really that hard, anyway." It was all he could do to stop himself from screaming.

"I was watching, Cody. You ran yourself silly for ninety minutes," his mom said.

"Not the whole practice, Mom. Come on." He wasn't getting anywhere. She would treat him like a baby for the rest of his life. He had an idea. "Kenneth and Luca are coming to pick me up," he said.

"You didn't tell me that," she said sharply.

A glimmer of hope? "I'll go for an hour and come back. They invited me — so it would be kinda rude not to go."

"I'm worried about you exhausting yourself," she said.

"You have a game tomorrow morning and . . ."

"I'll ride my bike over and come right back."

She looked at her watch. "I'll drive you."

"That won't work because they'll have their bikes and . . . how will they get back?"

"Sean, can you come here, please?" she called out.

His dad walked into the kitchen holding his cell phone. "What's up, Cheryl? I'm in the middle of something."

"Could you get off the phone for a minute and engage?" his mom said. "Cody's promised his friends from the Lions he'll go to City Hall Square. Apparently, there's some sort of event?"

"It's for UPW," his dad said. He held his hand up. "Can I call you back, Joel? I just have to deal with something. Sorry." He hung up.

"And UPW stands for?" she said.

"Ultra-Pure Water Company," he said. "Joel and I were just talking about it. Our company has put in a bid to work for them. They take water and purify it over and over until it has virtually no dirt or contaminates. Then they use the ultra-pure water to clean silicon microchips. These chips have thousands of tiny holes. After you make them, there's dirt in the holes, and you need the water to clean them."

"Ooookay," Cody's mom said. "Thanks for the nerd report, Sean. Anyway, I'd really like Cody to relax. He had a hard soccer practice and he has an early game tomorrow. We have to leave at eight to be there on time."

His dad put down his phone on the counter. Usually, his father gave in to his mom — maybe a bit less, recently. Could Cody get his dad on his side?

"I only want to go for an hour," Cody said. "Kenneth and Luca are coming over on their bikes — and I'll look lame if I don't go because I'm too tired — which I'm not."

His dad chuckled. "Do we really want our son to look lame?" he said.

His mom rolled her eyes. "I think you guys are about to gang up on me."

"No, we're not," his dad said softly. "It's only an hour. He goes and comes back. Lots of time to relax."

She let out a long sigh. "If you agree to only stay for an hour — okay," she said. "But be careful, and don't push it. The doctor told us you'd get tired. We have to make sure you're not getting run down."

"That was during my treatments, Mom," Cody said. "She didn't say that at the last checkup."

"You only finished treatments a few months ago," she said.

His dad got up. "If this crisis is over, can I get back to work? I have to get through a few emails and call Joel back."

"Saturday, Sean?" Cheryl said.

"I know — it's this UPW project. It's fairly big, and I'm behind the eight ball on it. Joel's gone crazy and piled the work on. I just need another hour — and then I'm all yours." He bowed to Cheryl.

Her face was stern — and then it relaxed. "Can I expect my hubby to take me out for coffee and a muffin?"

"I think that could happen — most definitely."

Cody knew his parents had been getting along better lately. They fought less, especially about him. If only he could get his mom to stop worrying so much. The doctor had said the cancer was gone — he was in remission.

The doorbell rang.

"I guess that's them?" Cody said tentatively.

"You can go — but be back by one o'clock," his mom said.

"For sure. Definitely by one . . . or one thirty."

"Don't push it, Cody," she said.

He knew that tone. "Just kidding, Momsy."

He opened the front door.

"I tried to ditch him. He keeps following me," Kenneth said, nodding at Luca.

"I thought we were playing hide-and-seek," Luca said. "Sorry."

"Like sorry is gonna cut it," Kenneth said. He turned to Cody. "You ready?"

Cody looked back over his shoulder. "I'm gonna get going now, Mom. Okay?"

She didn't answer. He closed the door behind him.

"So I checked out the standings after practice," Luca said. "The Storm have won five straight. Kills me to admit it — Timothy, Antonio, Tyler, and Michael have helped them, especially Timothy. He's scored eight goals since he bailed on the Lions."

"And John . . . ?" Kenneth's voice trailed off.

"Don't think he sees the field much," Luca said.

It was a quick ride to City Hall Square, about ten minutes. They locked their bikes to some parking meters and crossed the street to join the throng of people milling about. A large stage flanked by two tall speakers had been set up in front of the main building. A banner across the stage read UPW SAYS THANKS — TO A GREAT COMMUNITY. Food trucks lined the far side of the Square.

Kenneth sniffed the air. "I sense we're close to food," he said.

"Maybe we should ask those people eating pizza and hot dogs?" Luca said.

"Great idea, Mister Stupid — and end up totally lost," Kenneth said. "Follow me."

Kenneth led them into the crowd. Very soon they all had pizza slices, french fries, cotton candy, hot dogs, and a drink. Cody could barely carry it all.

"Where are the rest of the guys?" Cody asked.

Kenneth sniffed the air again. "Not sure. Let's go ask those strange-looking creatures over there." He nodded to the left — where Paulo, David, William, and Brandon were sitting on a patch of grass. They'd already gotten their food.

"Thanks for waiting," Kenneth said to them. "Everyone knows I'm a rude pig. But you guys? I'm shocked."

Kenneth plopped himself next to William. Cody took a spot off to the side.

"What's that banner over the stage all about?" Luca said. "What's a UPW?"

"I think it's the factory guys," David said.

Kenneth raised an eyebrow. "Why are you always so technical?"

"My dad told me they basically clean water," William said. "Maybe they're some sorta environmental company."

Cody didn't want to correct William in front of everyone.

Feedback crackled over the sound system, and he decided to let it go. It didn't matter.

A man walked out on the stage and took the microphone.

"That's Ian," Kenneth exclaimed.

Cody sat up. Why was Timothy's dad involved in this?

"Hi, everyone," Ian said, "and welcome to the UPW kickoff party. We're all excited to be working with such a first-class organization."

The speakers crackled again. Another man came out and tried to take the microphone from Ian.

"That's Mitch," Luca said.

Cody could only wonder what was going on. John's dad was part of this, too?

Ian pulled the microphone away and waved at Mitch dismissively with the back of his hand. Mitch backed up slowly and left the stage.

"I want to thank our good friends at UPW for this food and this great day," Ian said, "and for creating a hundred new jobs with the new water processing plant. And let's not forget the community centre. And, hold onto your hats, I just learned that UPW is donating twenty-five thousand dollars toward youth sports programming. So put your hands together for Carl Bornsteen, vice-president of international operations at UPW."

The people in the crowd clapped politely.

"I still don't get why UPW is doing all this," Paulo said.

Why did it matter? A new community centre and money for sports sounded good to Cody — not to mention this food.

"Let's get some ice cream before it's gone," William said, cuffing Brandon on the arm. "You ready, Paulo?"

"You go ahead. I've got another dog to finish off." Paulo held it up.

Brandon and William headed to the trucks.

Cody finished off his hot dog and dug out the last of his fries. He heard voices yelling.

"This is a cover up!

"Tell the truth, UPW!"

"Ultra-pure chemicals, not ultra-pure water!

Two women walked out of the crowd, escorted by a very tall police officer holding them by the forearms. One of the women kept trying to pull away. The officer barely noticed, he was so big. The woman's hair was striking — jet black with tight curls and cut very short. The other woman wasn't as tall, and had a pleasant, round face framed by soft, curly grey hair that hung just below her neck. Behind them came two girls, around Cody's age, escorted by another, smaller police officer making sure they kept up. One girl was the mirror image of the woman with the short hair, except her hair was tied up in lots of skinny braids and they bounced around as she walked. She was also very thin, almost slight — and she didn't look very happy. The other girl had a round face and dark brown eyes, with really thick, wavy hair that came to her shoulders.

Both girls were kind of pretty. The girl with the wavy hair was laughing and seemed to be enjoying herself. She pumped her sign up and down in the air. It read MY LAKE DOESN'T LIKE ARSENIC.

23

"You let go of my daughter," the short-haired woman said to the other police officer. "Is he hurting you, Mandy?"

"I'm fine, Mom," said the girl with the braids.

Mandy's mom struggled to get away.

"You best calm down, lady, or you'll be in serious trouble," the big officer growled.

"Candice, let's not make trouble," her friend said.

"I'm not making trouble, Sharon. He's the problem." Candice shook her arm violently. The big police officer rolled his eyes and let her go. She waved her sign at him. It read UPW: NO! LAKE TAWSON: YES!

"We have a right to protest. UPW can't buy freedom of speech, even if it is trying to buy city council," Candice said.

"You have the right to protest," the smaller officer said, "but you can't yell at the presenters on the stage."

"Don't tell me what I can or can't . . . "

"Are we going to have a problem?" the big cop said to Candice.

"No, we aren't," Sharon said. She reached over and lowered Candice's sign. "Can we stand here, officer?"

The smaller officer looked around. "I guess — but I don't understand what you're protesting. You don't like jobs — or community centres?"

"We don't like chemicals in our lake," Candice said, "or the lead or the copper or the arsenic."

"Okay, Candice," Sharon said. "We're here to express our opinion, not berate people."

Candice sighed. "Sharon, you're too nice."

"I can live with that," Sharon laughed. "We won't be disruptive, officers. We promise."

The big officer gave Candice a stern look, and he and his partner wandered back toward the stage.

"Thanks very much, Carl," Ian's voice rang out. "And now, I am overjoyed and totally stoked and over-the-top happy to introduce a man who needs no introduction. Our wonderful, perfect mayor — Mayor Winthrop."

The crowd clapped politely, again.

"No to UPW's dirty water!" Candice yelled, pumping her sign up and down. "Come on, girls. Don't let those cops intimidate you. C'mon, Talia. Hold that sign up."

The girl with the wavy hair raised her sign.

"You too, Mandy," Candice added.

Mandy's shoulders slumped, but she did it. Hers read ULTRA-PURE GARBAGE!

"Our lake is not for sale!" Candice chanted.

Kenneth slipped past Candice and Sharon and threw his arms around the two girls.

"As soon as I saw the cops I knew you two were involved," he said.

The two girls lowered their signs and followed Kenneth to where the boys were standing. Talia threw her arms out and gave Luca a big hug. Mandy pressed her sign in front of her chest and nodded.

"When did you guys turn to a life of crime?" Kenneth said.

Talia laughed. "Our moms are crazed. They won't even let us get any food."

"Brutal," Luca said. "You could have some of mine, only . . . I sorta ate it all."

Talia laughed. "You owe me — big time."

"Seriously, though. What's this all about?" Kenneth said.
Cody crept closer.

He listened as Talia repeated what his dad had told him earlier about UPW. Then she added some interesting facts. "Silicon chips are used in semi-conductors, which basically run computers and cell phones — everything that's technology. Lake Tawson's water is really clean to start with, so it's cheaper to turn it into ultra-pure water. UPW wants to build a factory there to make the ultra-pure water."

"And we hate that because . . . ?" Kenneth asked.

"Because silicon chips are full of chemicals and metal, and the waste from cleaning them with the ultra-pure water will end up in the lake," Talia answered. "UPW says it's perfectly safe. Candice says that's a total lie and Lake Tawson will be polluted. We get our drinking water from Lake Tawson. I don't want to hang out on a beach with a big factory on it."

Lake Tawson? Cody used to go there a lot when he was getting his treatments. It was a spot where he could get away from the hospital, into the fresh air, to feel the breeze off the lake — and just forget about being sick. He hadn't been back since his last treatment. Now the lake reminded him of his cancer, and he didn't need to be reminded of that. Still, he didn't want it to get polluted

The mayor continued with his speech. "Not only are we going to bring a ton of jobs to the community, we'll also have lots of spin-off businesses, with restaurants and trucking and . . . and we're going to attract more businesses . . . "

Candice stormed past Cody and headed toward the crowd. "The mayor is talking garbage, as usual," she fumed.

"I can't let him get away with it."

"Candice," Sharon called out. "Not a good idea." She ran after her.

"Your mom's really mellowed out," Kenneth said to Mandy.

"This time she's really lost it," Mandy said. "Our kitchen is like a war room. We have reports everywhere and newspaper articles cut out and lists of websites . . . " She shrugged. "Like Talia said, I don't like it either, but . . . Mom thinks chemicals were the reason . . . why Gavin . . . " Her voice trailed off.

Talia looked very serious all of a sudden. "It's more than that," she said quietly.

Mandy tapped the sign on the ground. "Maybe you're right."

Paulo joined them. "What's going on? We getting some ice cream?"

"Don't rub it in," Talia said.

"Hey, Cody," Kenneth said, "come meet the two best players from the team Luca and I were on last year. Talia was our leading scorer — and Mandy was a menace in the midfield. Naturally, with me on the team we won the championship, 'cause I'm so awesome and I basically dominated every game. Right?"

Talia scrunched her mouth to the side. "Are you sure you were on the team? I don't remember you."

"I'm a hero to these guys," Kenneth whispered. "It'll break their hearts to know I'm totally useless."

"We already do," Luca said.

"Did you tell them?" Kenneth glared at Talia.

27

"Well . . . you know . . . Facebook and stuff," Talia said. "So you guys have names?"

Kenneth introduced them. Red-faced, Cody managed a "hi". He hated meeting new people. He never knew what to say and it was way worse with girls. Paulo had no problem, and he began talking to Talia.

"Where are you from?" Talia said.

"Brazil."

"Wow. You speak without any accent," Talia said.

"I taught him English last week," Kenneth said.

"You really much good teacher-man," Paulo said.

Talia laughed, and even Mandy cracked a smile. Soon the conversation veered back to soccer.

"You guys gotta come to the park for some pick-up," Kenneth said to Talia.

"For sure," Luca echoed. "We usually play twice a week at least."

That stung. Cody had played with them a few times, but never twice a week.

"Sounds awesome." Talia turned to Mandy. "We're definitely into that, right?"

Mandy bounced her sign off her foot. "Yeah. Sure. I guess."

Brandon and William came out of the crowd with banana splits.

"Bros, it's actually all you can eat. You gotta get in there," William said.

"I assume this calls for extreme ninja behaviour," Kenneth said.

He and Luca dropped into a deep squat. They began

waddling duck-like toward the ice-cream trucks, with Talia laughing her head off.

"Let's get some ice cream," Talia said to Mandy. "Our moms are too busy yelling at the mayor to notice." She did the duck-waddle, too. Mandy raised her eyes to the sky and stood off to the side, arms crossed.

Paulo elbowed Cody.

"Let's do it, Cody. We need some ice cream in our lives," Paulo said.

He dropped into a squat and waddled fast to catch up.

Cody couldn't walk like that in public. He'd feel too stupid, especially with Mandy watching. He followed them slowly, at a distance. People were laughing and pointing. Either they didn't notice or didn't care, because Kenneth, Luca, Talia, and Paulo kept it up all the way to the trucks.

Cody threw his ice cream into the garbage. Waste of time lining up for so long. It was the cheap stuff that leaves a coating at the back of your throat. William and Brandon had gone off with their families about twenty minutes ago. He should've left then. Now he was stuck hanging with Kenneth, Luca, and Paulo and the two girls.

The guys would think he was a wuss if he told them why he really had to leave. He rolled his neck and looked longingly across the street at his bike. He wanted friends so badly sometimes; and yet, hanging with people was nerve-wracking. He cleared his throat.

"Hey, Luca, I sorta gotta get going," Cody said.

Luca didn't hear him. He, along with everyone else, was listening to Kenneth's story.

"I told the principal that I really wanted to finish the

project, but I couldn't let a kitten stay up in that tree — and that's why I handed it in late."

"You had no choice," Luca said. "You can't leave an itty-bitty kitten in a tree."

"Exactly," Kenneth said. "That's why it's the perfect animal to use when you want to get out of a detention."

Cody bit the inside of his lip in frustration. His mom would freak out. It had been way over an hour. She'd probably drive over — just to humiliate him. He needed to get this done. He cleared his throat louder this time and stepped forward.

"Yeah, so I gotta get going," Cody said.

No one paid any attention — again. The boys were all looking over his shoulder.

"Uhmm . . . Anyway . . . This has been cool . . . I mean fun . . . "

Kenneth's jaw was set and his eyes were cold. An icy shiver ran down Cody's back. What had he done? Was he mad he didn't do that stupid walk? Cody looked at Kenneth.

"Sorry about . . . "

"Turn around, Cody," Paulo said. He too looked very serious.

Cody turned around — and instantly forgot about his mom or Kenneth's scowl. Five guys were walking toward them — the very same guys who'd quit the Lions and joined the Storm.

Timothy had a blue and white baseball cap on, with THE STORM written across the top. He wore a Lacoste shirt, designer jeans, and Oakley sunglasses.

"Hey, Antonio, Eggy's got some fuzz on his head now," Timothy said.

"Now he's Fuzz Head," John said, giggling to himself.

"Timothy, I gotta admit I'm disappointed to see you. I thought you'd been run over by a truck," Kenneth said.

"I'll be running you over tomorrow at the game, don't worry," Timothy said, and his friends laughed.

John held out his fist. Timothy left him hanging.

"It's good we're playing you," Timothy continued. "It'll be a warm-up for when we play United next week."

United was the first-place team.

"It'll be a warm-up for the Storm to lose 10–0," Paulo said.

"Jungle Boy's learned some English?" Antonio said.

"Here's some English for you, Jungle Boy," Timothy said. "Go Home!"

Paulo's fists balled. "Make me."

Talia elbowed Luca. "Who's the clown?" she said.

"This clown and his clown friends used to play on the Lions," Luca said. "That's Timothy. Thinks he's a striker. Next door is John — a kinda useless player, so be sensitive."

"Their dads used to be the Lions' managers. Timothy's dad was the team sponsor, too," Kenneth said. "The other three losers are Antonio, Tyler, and Michael. We lost every game when they were on our team. Then they left, and we've won six straight and a tournament. Coincidence?"

"The Storm won every league game since we joined, too, freak," Antonio said.

"Sorry to have to bring out the big guns," Kenneth

said, "but you forced me. I know you are, but what am I?"

Antonio waved Kenneth off and stepped toward Cody. "You ready to go, Egg-Head? You act all tough when there's a referee around to protect you. Let's see if you're so tough now."

Cody tried not to panic. Antonio was even bigger than Timothy.

"I don't remember asking you to join the conversation," Mandy said.

Cody couldn't believe she said that.

"*Ya mon*," Timothy said in a fake Jamaican accent. "Nice braids, Rasta girl. Now go get me a beef patty. I'm hungry."

Mandy's head jerked back as if she'd been slapped. Cody could barely believe his ears. He wanted to say something, but the others beat him to it.

"Get lost," Talia said.

"He can't," Luca said. "He's too dumb."

"I'd forgotten how lame you guys are," Timothy said.

"I'd forgotten how much I love kicking your butts — like the last time we played," Luca said.

The boys lined up across from each other. Cody gave up on getting in on the trash talk.

"Did I mention my dad's company is building the community centre?" Timothy said. "Suck up to me and maybe I'll let you look through the doors."

John held his hand up for a high-five. Timothy ignored him.

Kenneth slapped his forehead. "I totally forgot to ask. How are those new diapers working out for you?" he said to Timothy. "I heard your last brand leaked."

Antonio took a step forward and shoved Kenneth with two hands. Luca shoved him back.

"Not here, bro," Timothy said, an arm outstretched across Antonio's chest. "Our dads will be mad if there's a fight." He tilted his chin up. "It's been fun seeing so many losers together in one place, like a loser convention, but we gotta go to a special ceremony inside City Hall — invitation only."

"No stupid guys allowed — or ugly girls," Michael said.

"See ya, Jungle Boy," John said.

"And I'll be crackin' your Egg-Head tomorrow," Antonio said to Cody.

"You can't leave already," Kenneth groaned. "We hardly had a chance to talk."

"I so want to shut that big mouth of yours up," Timothy said. "I'm definitely gonna do it, too. Definitely."

"You're definitely gonna have to repeat grade three — I'm definite about that," Kenneth responded.

"I wanna hear from Humpty Dumpty," Antonio said. "Eggs have a right to talk, too."

Cody's stomach felt like he'd eaten a bowling ball and his throat was totally dry. He just wasn't good at dissing.

"We'll see how tough you are tomorrow when the Lions win by five goals," Mandy said.

Antonio began to laugh and he elbowed Tyler in the ribs. "When did Humpty's voice get all girly on him?"

"He plays like a girl, so that makes sense," Tyler said.

"What does that even mean?" Paulo said disgustedly.

"Means you shouldn't be in our country, Jungle Boy. And you, too, Rasta Girl. And Humpty's a total wuss,"

Timothy said. "Let's roll, guys. There's a private party with our names on it."

Timothy turned and left, with the others following him.

"Why's the world so beautiful when they're not around?" Kenneth said.

"Because they suck the joy out of life?" Luca said.

"That is correct, young man," Kenneth said.

"Let's hear it for the words *used to play on our team*," Luca said.

"Hip-hip-hooray! Paulo, Kenneth, and Luca cheered.

Cody kept quiet — way too late to dis them now.

"So . . . what was that?" Talia asked.

"It would take days to explain," Kenneth said.

"How about a short summary?" Talia said.

"Hmm." Kenneth rubbed his chin with his hand. "Their dads, Ian and Mitch, had me, Luca, and Cody stapled to the bench as subs. Then Trevor, our coach, took over the team and made us starters. Those guys didn't like it and quit. Now they play for the Storm."

"The only problem is we only have eleven players," Luca said.

"Eleven! What if someone gets hurt — or goes on vacation?" Talia said.

"Or someone gets carried away with knitting a sweater and misses a bunch of games?" Luca said. He pulled on Kenneth's shirt. "Did I say that out loud?"

"You did," Kenneth said. "But we're totally behind you on the sweater project."

"The sweater is way bigger than a stupid soccer team," Paulo said.

Cody almost said, "We can't let Luca get cold." He worried it wasn't funny, though, and kept quiet.

Luca pretended to cry. "You guys are all getting knitted socks at the team banquet."

"Sounds a bit itchy," Kenneth said. "Maybe you should focus on the sweater."

"Are you guys done?" Talia said.

Kenneth and Luca nodded.

"We're absolutely coming to watch the game tomorrow," Talia said. "Those guys are too obnoxious to live. What time?"

"Ten thirty."

Mandy suddenly broke away from the group. "Mom!" she called out.

The big cop was holding Candice by the arm. Sharon walked beside them.

"Next time I'll throw you in the wagon and take you to the station," he said to Candice. "You can't throw things at the mayor."

"So it's okay for him to kill children with chemicals?" Candice yelled.

"I think we should leave," Sharon said. She put an arm around Candice's shoulders. "Sorry, officer. We're going to go now."

"Good," he huffed and folded his arms.

"We aren't leaving until we . . . "

"Hush," Sharon said to Candice.

For a moment Candice looked about to burst into tears. "We aren't giving up," Candice said to the police officer. "We're coming back — with five hundred people next time. This is the beginning. We're only getting organized. We'll have half the town protesting soon enough."

"I'm sure you will," the officer grinned.

"UPW can't buy off everyone. There are too many honest people in this town for that." Candice cupped her hands around her mouth. "Scream if you love Lake Tawson!" she cried.

The policeman snickered. "Whatever. No more throwing things at the mayor, okay? You'll go to jail if I see that again."

"The mayor should be in jail for supporting UPW," Candice said.

The officer rolled his eyes and walked off.

"Mom, can we go already?" Mandy said. "No one cares. I mean look around."

Everyone was crowded around the food trucks or the stage.

"Gavin was deeply committed to the environment," Candice said, her voice choked with emotion. "I won't let another child be hurt by toxic chemicals, not while I'm still alive, anyway. I expect more from you, Mandy."

Mandy's lips pressed together tightly. Cody could tell by the way Talia, Kenneth, and Luca looked at each other that this Gavin was very important.

"It's been a tiring day," Sharon said. "Why don't we go to my place and talk about how to organize things."

"Sounds good, Mom," Talia said.

Candice let the air seep slowly through her lips. "Okay, I'll be a good girl. Let's go," she said.

Candice and Sharon began to walk across the Square.

"See you tomorrow at the game — and good luck," Talia said to them. "Kick some Storm butt."

"Consider it done, with an extra butt-kick because it feels so good," Kenneth said.

Talia laughed and she and Mandy set off after their moms. The boys all seemed lost in their own thoughts for a moment.

"I guess I better get going too," Cody said finally. "We're . . . my parents are going out . . . I mean we're all going out, so . . . I guess . . . I gotta go."

Kenneth held a hand out. Cody hesitated. This always seemed forced. He slapped his hand, and then slapped Luca and Paulo's.

Cody crossed the street to get his bike. He needed to find out more about UPW. But first he was gonna have to deal with a far more serious problem — his mom. He'd stayed way too long.

Trevor jabbed his marker onto the whiteboard. "What are the three rules?" He pointed to Cody. "Rule one?"

"Support in triangles."

"Rule two?"

"Possession is power."

"Three?"

"Identify the weakness and attack."

Trevor looked pleased. "You get an A, Cody." He put the cap on the marker. "Three players around the ball, at the right distance apart, means the player with the ball has choices. It's impossible for one defender to get the ball. Attack in threes, in triangles, and the ball goes to the player farthest away. The defender will have to run. To form the triangles you have to work hard in support. To keep the ball you have to be patient and no low-percentage passes.

To score you have to have the killer instinct. Ball possession is not an excuse to go to sleep. Stay aggressive."

The referee blew his whistle.

"Kenneth, go out for the coin toss," Trevor said.

"What d'ya want?" Kenneth said.

"I'd rather have the far end in the second half. It's windy. Let them kick off."

"You got it," Kenneth said, flashing a pair of finger guns.

"Having only eleven guys makes the starting lineup easier to figure out, I grant you that," Trevor said. He held up the whiteboard. "We'll start with a 4-3-1-2. Luca, William, Jacob, and Austin on the back line. Brandon, Kenneth, and Ryan in midfield. Paulo will play behind Cody and Jordan. On the attack, look for Paulo, with midfielders supporting. Remember, lots of overlapping, and lots of pressure on the ball."

Cody   Jordan

Paulo

Brandon Kenneth Ryan

Luca William Jacob Austin

David

Kenneth jogged back. "They kick off. We got the end you wanted. Let's put it in, boys." He extended his hand and everyone put theirs on top. "Lions on three," he yelled. "One, two, three . . . "

The boys let out a roar.

Cody peeled off, windmilling his arms, more to calm his nerves than to loosen up. Their disastrous 0–7 start to the season meant they couldn't afford to lose another game or the playoffs would be tough to make. An arm draped over his shoulders.

"We run — we pass — we crush," Paulo said, deadly earnest. He gave Cody's head a rub and set off to camp out to the left of the circle. Paulo's skills had quickly won Trevor's trust and he had the green light to play basically wherever he wanted.

Timothy and a kid Cody didn't know strolled toward the ball. John was on the sidelines — not a starter on this team, it seemed. Antonio was inside right back. Michael and Tyler were in the midfield. It would be a tough battle to break through their defence.

"That's the guy," Timothy said in a mocking tone, elbowing number nine beside him. "The one and only Egg-Head. Let's see if we can crack him open." Number nine glowered menacingly.

Show no fear, Cody told himself. *It's just talk.* A chill ran down his back and his stomach got tight. He just wanted to play soccer.

"There's the guy who needs his daddy to buy him a team so he can play," Paulo said.

"There's Jungle Boy who needs to get a bunch of

41

bananas and go home," Timothy said. He made a monkey sound and scratched his armpits.

"You should be imitating a chicken," Paulo said, a dark edge to his voice. "When it gets down to it, you always get scared and run away."

The referee blew his whistle and waved his arm in the air to signal the start of play.

"Our ball all game," Kenneth called out from midfield.

Timothy nudged the ball to number nine, who rolled it to his centre midfielder. Cody ran forward.

"Ooof," he gasped. Timothy's elbow dug into his ribs. Cody staggered and dropped to one knee.

The Storm midfielder swung the ball wide right. The ref drifted up field. With Cody down Timothy had tons of room. He received a pass and one-timed it to his right winger. The Storm pressed forward on the attack. Cody stood up.

"That's a red card," Cody shouted at the referee, and he began to run after the ball.

"Cody! Stay up with Jordan!" Trevor yelled at him.

Cody skidded to a stop. He was so mad his ears hurt. Trevor was right. A striker can't run all over the place. He had to stay up for the attack. But how'd the ref miss that elbow? It was right in front of him.

Luca confronted the Storm winger on the flank. The winger passed square to Timothy. True to form he faked a pass back and bulled his way toward the net. William wasn't fooled and stood firm. Timothy did a good job spinning to his right and firing a right-footed bullet at the top corner. David dove across smartly to catch the ball. The acrobatic goalie rolled on his shoulder and was up in a flash, delivering the ball to Luca near the sideline.

Luca carried it forward and sent a pass to Brandon. Kenneth came over to support, as did Cody. Brandon punched it to him, and Cody spun inside thinking he'd feed Paulo on the break.

"Not quite, Eggy," Antonio growled.

Next thing he knew, Cody lay on the ground, holding his calf where Antonio had kneed him. The whistle stopped play.

"Free kick, Lions," the referee said. "Be careful, number four," he said to Antonio. "Next one will earn you a card." Cody rubbed his calf. "You okay, number ten?" he said.

"That should be the second red card, ref," Cody said.

The referee shrugged and blew his whistle. He backed up, windmilling his arm vigorously.

"Head to the right and I'll look for you," Paulo said to Cody.

Cody nodded and ran to a spot on the right about ten metres from the box. He needed to be on his guard. He was going to be a target this game. The referee obviously wasn't going to protect him.

Earlier in the year, the Lions would've booted the ball downfield — and lose it as often as not. This time, Kenneth flicked it to Paulo, who skidded up the left side, with Brandon and Jordan in support. That brought a smile to Cody's face. He bet Trevor was smiling, too — a perfect triangle. Two Storm defenders chased the ball, but Paulo, Brandon, and Jordan kept it moving too fast for them to gain possession.

Cody was tempted to join in. Trevor had told them the magic number was three — not four. The fourth guy was supposed to wait for an opening to attack. To do that he had to run. So run he did, in between the outside midfielder and back, then a fake run to goal to test the backline. Paulo switched it up and sent it to Kenneth. Cody got on his horse and raced to an opening just outside the box. Like Trevor said, spot the weakness and attack. A quick pass and Cody could dart in either direction to get a clear look on goal.

A flash of pain made Cody crumple to the ground holding his right foot. One of the Storm centre backs had stomped him with his cleats.

"What's with that?" Kenneth yelled. He passed right to Ryan.

"Get up," the referee said to Cody, "and quit your acting. Last warning. Next flop is a yellow."

Cody groaned and got to his feet. Acting? The guy tried to break his foot.

Ryan gave it back to Kenneth. He took it left and distributed the ball to Jordan, who sent it to Paulo. He and Brandon passed to each other a few times and then the ball ended up back with Jordan sneaking down the left flank. Antonio charged him with a slide tackle and took Jordan's feet out from under him, knocking the ball out of bounds.

The whistle blew. "Free kick, Lions."

"I got the ball first," Antonio fumed.

The referee pointed to goal. It was a direct kick, but from that angle it would be tough to put the ball on net.

Cody pressed wide for the cross, jockeying with a Storm defender for position. Jordan rolled the ball back to Paulo — so much for the cross.

"Our ball," Kenneth yelled. He accepted a pass from Paulo, and in turn passed it back to Luca.

"Keep running, Lions," William said.

"Hold onto the ball," Paulo said.

Cody wanted to add they needed to stay aggressive.

He didn't, and instead, ran to the right. For the rest of the half he basically ran himself ragged. He got a few good looks, but each time their goalie was up to the challenge. Cody was glad to hear the half-time whistle. He needed a rest.

Cody jogged to the sidelines and took a seat on the grass. Kenneth, Luca, and Paulo sat next to him.

"Good half," Trevor said. "Grab some water and something to eat if you're hungry. Then gather around."

"Ref's asleep," Paulo said. "They should've had ten yellow cards by now — and a few reds."

"Did you check out Austin?" Kenneth said. "He plowed that guy over and then got to trash talking. I mean, we're talkin' about Austin. I don't think I've heard him say ten words all season."

"Team toughness was huge," Luca said.

"Maybe too huge," Kenneth said. "You, me, Paulo, and William have yellows."

"Luca's yellow card was sweet, though," Paulo said.

"Bad call," Luca said. "My shoulder slipped and hit Timothy in the chest."

"Timothy deserves an Oscar for best supporting jerk

trying to convince the ref to give you a red card," Kenneth said.

"That's their strategy," Paulo said. "They want us to do something stupid because we don't have subs."

"You must be made of ice," Luca said to Cody. "They're fouling you every time you touch the ball. I would've lost it by now."

"You almost got that left-footer to go," Kenneth said to Cody.

Paulo had broken free and fed him a sweet pass into the box. Cody had struck the ball cleanly — and had to endure a solid clout from Antonio — only to see the goalie get his right hand on the ball and deflect it a few centimetres wide of the post. Otherwise, the game had been really tight, with no one getting a great chance. Timothy had almost scored from in close, but David had punched it over the bar.

"Listen up, lads," Trevor said.

The boys swung around.

"Not a bad first half," Trevor said. "Fairly chippy. From the look of it they're trying to intimidate. Remember — never back down on the soccer pitch."

Kenneth raised his hand.

"Yes?" Trevor said.

"What does backing down mean?" Kenneth asked.

Trevor chuckled. "Good question. I don't know either. Anyway, we have to be careful. No more yellows, please. And those of you with yellows, keep in mind, you get one more and you're out of this game and the next. The league has an automatic one-game suspension for any red cards.

With only eleven players, obviously that would be a bad thing."

"Play hard, but walk away from confrontations," Leandro said. "It's easy to lose your temper. A real player knows his emotions are less important than the team."

Cody listened intently. Paulo's father had a way of saying the right thing at the right time. The Lions had played tough, for sure. The yellow cards meant that toughness had to be controlled in the second half.

"The ball possession is good," Trevor said, "so kudos for that. Ball movement is not so good. Short, lateral passes between two players won't do much. It's static. You can't penetrate their zone that way."

"Ball control is not the same as being passive," Leandro

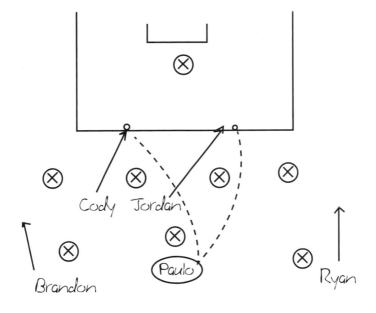

Paulo passing inside to Cody or Jordan

47

said. He quickly sketched a play on the whiteboard. "We aren't attacking — except that one chance by Cody. More of that. Kill them in the middle. Cody and Jordan need to angle into space. The chances will come from there."

This new style was sure more complicated than the kick-and-chase game Cody was used to.

"Keep hydrating," Trevor said, "and let's get fired up for the second half."

"I'm gonna stretch my leg out," Cody said to his teammates. "I can feel it tightening up."

"Fine — be that way," Kenneth said with a scowl.

Cody flushed. Maybe he should be talking strategy?

Kenneth rolled his eyes. "I'm sorry, bro. It's too easy sometimes."

"It's like being mean to a puppy," Luca said.

Cody was bewildered.

"He's joking," Paulo grinned.

Cody felt ridiculously gullible. "I knew that . . . I just wanted . . . to make you feel good about yourself." He looked on helplessly.

"You . . . um . . . gonna stretch your leg?" Kenneth said.

Cody nodded and shifted over a few metres. When would he learn? Kenneth, Luca, and Paulo began talking about the Storm. He caught fragments.

". . . ref's unreal."

". . . Timothy should've been gone . . . "

". . . we gotta . . . no choice . . . "

They laughed, and Luca and Kenneth slapped hands. Cody straightened his legs and bent over to touch his toes. His calves loosened. At the back of his right leg he could still feel the spot where they'd operated.

"Make it burn," a girl's voice said.

It was Mandy.

Cody jumped up. "My . . . leg gets tight."

"I don't want to bug you," she said. "I'm just here with Talia — she's over there."

Talia was sitting cross-legged on the ground, drinking from a water bottle.

"I noticed the Storm's outside right back, number three," Mandy said. "He keeps drifting into the middle — like he gets bored. Hang outside. If someone feeds you the ball you should be able to take it wide. Worst thing is he brings you down for a free kick."

She was right. He'd noticed that, too. Still, it was irritating to be told about it, as if he'd never played before. "Okay. I'll look for it. Coach has another strategy, kinda complicated, so . . ."

He wasn't making sense.

"Complicated strategies? Sounds serious." Her half-smile made it hard for him to know if she was kidding. She folded her arms across her chest. "You're doing good. You work hard, I'll give you that. Now just go after that right back and score. You gotta beat these guys. They're such . . . jerks."

"Okay, Lions. Let's get out there!" Trevor yelled. He clapped with his clipboard.

"Yo, Cody. You stretched out?" Kenneth said.

He'd stretched for two seconds. "Yeah. I'm good."

"So . . . you coming or what?"

"Good luck," Mandy whispered, with a giggle.

Cody jogged back onto the pitch. The Storm's number three took his place at right back.

Attack outside? Probably worth a try.

He ran over to Paulo. "Look for me over on the left. I wanna go after that number three."

Paulo nodded. "I'll get it to you."

The ref placed the ball at centre. He wanted to score so much it hurt — more than his calf or foot combined — to show to Timothy and his crew — and Mandy — what Cody Dorsett was all about.

Austin squared the ball to Jacob near the right sideline. He knocked it up to Ryan. Kenneth came over. Paulo was on that side already. Normally, Cody would go to the left for a cross — this triangle thing confused him, though. Should he go make a triangle with Paulo and Kenneth, or let Paulo, Kenneth, and Ryan make the triangle?

"Move, Cody!" Trevor barked.

"Move, Cody! Do something," Antonio mimicked in a high-pitched voice. He jabbed Cody with his elbow as he passed by.

Cody ignored him — although the elbowing hurt. He needed to move — but where? He headed toward the ball.

"No!" Trevor shouted, pointing in the opposite direction.

Cody spun on his heels and raced back, utterly confused.

"You lost? Need your mommy?" Michael snickered.

"Shut up," Cody snapped.

"Eggy's getting all fussy," Antonio said.

Cody rolled his eyes. Always the same thing from these guys.

Cody set up not far from the corner of the box on the left, about even with the back line. The Storm's number three marked him. Ryan had the ball just over centre. Jordan made a run and Ryan gave it to him, but in the face of two Storm defenders Jordan backtracked. After a few passes the ball ended up on Kenneth's foot, at centre, about fifteen metres from the right sideline. Cody ran up and back, darted into the box, sprinted wide left — all for nothing. The Lions continued to control the play, but they couldn't move it forward.

"Come on, Lions! Play soccer! I'm bored to death!" Ian yelled. He threw his hands up in the air. A group of men around him, all wearing Storm baseball caps and shirts with tornadoes on the front, began chirping Trevor.

"Teach your boys to play like men."

"They scared to score?"

"Most boring game I've ever seen."

Paulo had the ball, Kenneth and Jordan in support, with Ryan out wide on the flank. Paulo looked over his shoulder a few times, which raised Cody's hopes he might actually see a cross. It didn't happen. Paulo shifted the ball to the centre of the field to Kenneth. Cody jogged to the left sidelines. The Storm's number three stepped up to mark him again. Paulo looked his way. Kenneth passed to Paulo. Kenneth looked over this time. Still no cross. The ball ping-ponged between Paulo and Kenneth a few more times, and every so often one of them would glance his way.

Cody suddenly got it. The Storm's number three had drifted inside. Paulo and Kenneth were setting it up. Cody began to breathe hard, as if he were really tired. He casually took a few more steps left. Paulo dribbled to the left, still in the middle of the field, about halfway between centre and the box. Kenneth sprinted forward, catching the midfielder marking him off guard. Paulo angled the pass, and Kenneth took it without breaking stride. Cody tensed, readying himself.

Kenneth took one step and lofted the ball into the box in his direction. Cody took off like a freight train and brought the ball down with his left foot. Out of the corner of his eye he saw Antonio cutting over full tilt. He didn't have much time. The goalie crouched down and opened his legs and arms wide. Cody reared back and drove the ball. The goalie stuck out his right foot. Antonio lowered his shoulder.

Cody went flying, skidding across the grass on his side. Whatever pain he might have felt disappeared when he heard the whistle.

He'd scored!

Kenneth looked down at him, his hand out. "The mailman delivers — as always," he said.

Cody took Kenneth's hand and pulled himself up.

Antonio walked away without a word.

"Awesome strike," Jordan said.

"No way he was gonna stop that," Paulo said.

Kenneth held his hand down low. Cody gave it an emphatic slap. Brandon and Ryan held their hands out and he slapped them. Then they jogged back to their end in a pack. The back line was waiting.

"I almost missed the goal," Luca said. "You guys had the ball so long I started reading a book. Nicely done, number ten."

Cody and Luca slapped hands.

"Maybe they'll stick to soccer now and forget the cheap shots," Cody said.

"This ain't over," Paulo said. "I think a few guys over there don't like us."

The referee planted the ball at centre.

"Hey, ref," Kenneth said. "Kinda think their number four threw a body check on that goal, no?"

"You guys focus on the game; I'll focus on refereeing; and there won't be a problem, okay?"

Kenneth jogged back to his position. "He's actually a real fun guy," he whispered to Cody and Paulo.

Paulo gave Cody a pat on the back. "We gotta add one, and then about four more," Paulo said. "This needs to be a slaughter."

The whistle blew and Timothy passed to number nine. He faked a pass wide right, then sent it to his mid-half. Timothy didn't move. Cody took a few paces forward. Jordan had taken the initiative to pressure.

"You get a nice pep talk from your ugly Rasta girl-friend?" Timothy said, with a huge grin.

Cody had never hated someone — until he'd met Timothy. The guy was just . . . a jerk. How much would he love to rip him apart with a dis? He thought about it — maybe something about Timothy's red hair?

"Just remember to bring a leash next time you take her for a walk," Timothy said. "Those island girls are savage."

No guy should talk like that about a girl.

Cody accelerated forward. All he could see was Timothy's mocking face. That idiotic smile that drove him crazy.

Cody's mind went blank. He drove his shoulder into Timothy's chest. Timothy crumpled and did a backward somersault. Cody stumbled to catch his balance, half in shock at what he'd done — and half loving it. Finally! He should've done that at the first Lions tryout when Timothy chirped him.

The outside right midfielder had the ball near the sideline. Cody figured he'd feed it back. He ran toward the Storm goal.

TWEET!

He turned around.

Timothy was still lying on the ground, propped up on an elbow, a huge grin plastered across his face. The referee was running over, his right hand over his head.

Cody felt dizzy, as if all the blood had rushed to his feet. There it was, up in the air for all to see — a red card. He'd never even gotten a yellow card before this season. He'd never even gotten a detention at school.

"He's been chirping me all game," Cody stuttered.

The ref stuffed the red card back in his shirt pocket and thumbed over his shoulder. He took out a notebook and began writing in it.

A sick feeling rose up from Cody's stomach. "I couldn't get out of the way . . . "

The referee ignored him.

Paulo came over, eyes downcast, along with Kenneth.

"We'll defend the lead, don't worry," Paulo said.

Kenneth put his hand on Cody's shoulder. "It's always nice to see Timothy on his butt," he said.

TWEET!

"Get off the field, number ten. I don't want to have to ask again," the ref said.

"Yeah, off the field," Timothy said. He got to his knees. "You're not playing anymore."

Kenneth and Paulo looked glumly at the Storm goal. Luca's arms hung limply by his sides. Jordan and Brandon had their heads together, whispering. Brandon's head shook slowly from side to side. David leaned against a goalpost. Cody began to walk off, every step a torture. It felt like ten minutes to get to the sideline. The Lions parents were quiet. His mom's arms were tight across her chest, her eyes fixed on him.

He'd totally messed up, let everyone down. The Lions would have to finish the game with only ten players.

"You should be outta the league for that hack job!" Ian bellowed.

"Brutal play," John said. "Total cheap shot."

"Worst play I've ever seen," Mitch said.

The Storm dads muttered and pointed at him.

Trevor escorted him off the field. "So what was that all about?" he said quietly.

Cody was so angry — at himself — at Timothy — it was all he could do to keep from crying.

"Talk to me, Cody," Trevor said.

Mandy stood close by. She seemed totally shocked.

He couldn't tell him the truth, not with her listening.

"Cody, I need an explanation," Trevor said, this time with a bit of sharpness in his voice. "A red card means you miss the next game, and they might suspend you, too. What gives?"

Cody tried to think of a reasonable explanation. He looked over at Mandy. She opened her eyes wide — and then smiled.

"I lost it," Cody said. "Sorry. I . . . It was stupid. He said something about me. He's said it a hundred times so I don't know why it got to me. I'm sorry. I just lost it."

Trevor rubbed his chin. "Hopefully, this will be a lesson. When you hold things in and don't deal with them, they tend to explode, especially when it comes to feelings. Think about it, okay, and we can talk later." He cupped his hands around his mouth. "Pressure on the ball, Ryan. Back him up, Austin."

"I'm getting that kid suspended for the rest of the season," Ian said loudly.

"He should be," Mitch agreed.

Cody crouched down and picked at the grass. He was sure Mandy was looking at him, but he didn't want to talk to her right now. He didn't want to talk to anyone.

Luca kicked the ball down the field. A Storm midfielder got it and swung it wide left. Could the boys hold on? With only ten men they wouldn't be able to play the ball possession game. It was defend and hope for the best.

He could only hope for the best, too. Missing one game was bad. What if the league suspended him for more? What if they suspended him for the rest of the season?

Cody lay his head on his arm and tapped the return key.

In 1840, a young man named Percival Elliot Tawson arrived in the area to prospect for gold.

He scanned the rest of the webpage quickly. Apparently, Lake Tawson was named after Percival. He'd fallen in love with a girl named Charlotte who was from a rich family. Percival came to Lake Tawson to find gold. His plan was to strike it rich and go back and marry Charlotte. One morning Percival was found dead by the shore, stabbed in the heart. That got Cody's attention. He began to read more closely. An unfinished letter was found in Percival's jacket pocket. The last line read, "I haven't found any gold yet, Charlotte, but I shan't give up, not while I have a single breath left in my body — for hope is still glittering in my soul — and we will be together again one day."

"There's a guy who doesn't give up easy," Cody said to himself.

His parents had gone to his Auntie Beth's for brunch. He'd been left behind — as part of being grounded for his red card. Probably got off lucky. His mom yelled at him the entire drive home from the game. He even had to eat dinner in his bedroom and go straight to bed afterwards. He didn't sleep for hours, though. He kept going over it. Why'd he run into Timothy? Was it because of what Timothy said about Mandy? But Cody barely knew her.

He clicked on another website. UPW was a huge company — massive. It had water factories all over the world — and there were entire websites hating on them.

UPW sued by environmental group in Malaysia.

Cody turned the computer off — enough. He had to get out of the house. He'd been cooped up all day. He reached down and rubbed the back of his right leg. It didn't hurt at all. Cody went upstairs, put his shoes on, grabbed a ball from the closet, and headed outside to the park. His mom had given him permission to go there for one hour — max!

Cody dropped the ball on the sidewalk and began dribbling down the street. He and his dad had another argument about UPW. Cody had lost his temper a bit and yelled. He wasn't sure why he did that either. He'd read enough about ultra-pure water to know it wasn't black-and-white. There were tons of scientific facts and figures on both sides of the argument. Yet, whenever he talked to his dad about it he became a wild child. He even accused his dad of wanting to turn Lake Tawson into a sewer.

That had earned him another day of being grounded.

Cody walked through the trees surrounding the park. He ran to the open field, cutting left and right, knocking the ball with the outsides of his feet. It was getting hot. He peeled off his sweatshirt, and then tried to see how many times he could bounce the ball in the air with his feet.

"Ach," he cried, as the ball squibbed off to the side. He'd gotten to ten.

"Woohoo!"

"Go, Cody, go!"

"Hello, Mister Fancy Feet!"

Kenneth, Paulo, and Luca appeared through the trees, and next to them, Talia and Mandy. Cody tried to laugh it off, waving and running for the ball. He didn't feel like laughing. They must think he was bit dorky — messing up an easy thing like that. Paulo could do it a hundred times on each foot.

He'd forgotten about Kenneth asking the girls to play. That was why they were here. Now he really looked dorky — by himself in the park.

"We stopped by your place. No one was there," Kenneth said.

"We figured you'd be here," Luca added.

That surprised him. Maybe they'd texted him when he was busy looking up info on Lake Tawson and UPW. "I kinda got grounded for a couple of days — red card and all." He paused, and then decided to get it over with. "Did you read Trevor's email this morning?"

Paulo made a sour face. "The league is being totally bogus. We should be able to start a game with ten players."

"You can play with ten. Why not start the game with ten?" Luca said.

"But the rule is you have to have eleven players for the kickoff," Talia said.

Kenneth's head swivelled her way. "If you're going to be sensible and reasonable, then you can go home right now, young lady."

"Oh, sorry. I meant the league is being stupid for following the rules," Talia said.

"We only have to forfeit one game," Paulo said.

"I was looking at the standings," Luca said. "We're sorta under the gun. We lose another game and it'll be tough for us to make the playoffs."

"Lucky we pulled out a point against the Storm," Kenneth said.

Cody dug his nails into his palms. Timothy had tied the game up mid-way through the second half. Brutal.

"What happened, anyway?" Kenneth said to Cody. "There was the kickoff and then I saw you plow into him."

Mandy had tied her braids into a big bun. How could Timothy say she was ugly? He was such a jerk. Cody felt himself getting mad.

"It was the usual," he said. "Not sure why I did it. Just did."

"If we're going to forfeit a game, then knocking Timothy on his butt's as good a reason as any," Kenneth said.

"Amen, brother," Luca said.

"Let's play already," Kenneth said. He toe dragged the ball away from Cody. "Me and the ladies will take on you three pylons."

"Shouldn't we even it up?" Cody said.

Mandy lowered her eyelids halfway and put her hands on her hips and looked straight at him. His comment obviously wasn't appreciated. Fortunately, Kenneth saved him.

"He meant we should change teams every few goals," he said, kicking the ball to Luca. "You guys can start."

Mandy smirked and backtracked to her side. She and Kenneth threw their sweatshirts down for posts. Paulo and Luca did the same on the other side. Cody tossed his sweatshirt on Paulo's. Luca gave the ball to Paulo who chipped it ahead for Cody. Mandy shifted to cover him. Perhaps still unnerved, or just nervous playing against girls, he mishandled the ball and it bounced off his toe and rolled a few feet away. Mandy was on it like a flash. She poked it past Cody and rolled the ball between Paulo and Luca for a goal.

She spun around. "Maybe we should even it up now?" she said sweetly to Cody.

Cody kicked at the ground.

"That was a practice," Paulo said. He retrieved the ball and back-heeled it to Luca. Again, the ball came to Cody.

"Redeem yourself, bro," Luca said.

Talia and Kenneth spread out to the left. Mandy was on him again. She was so thin it didn't seem fair that she had to cover him. He decided to dribble past her, so she'd show him some respect. He faked a right-footed knock inside to Luca, and nudged the ball with the outside of his left. Mandy didn't move. She stood fairly square to him. There was room between her legs, however. This was almost too easy. He kicked the ball and began to run around her to her right.

Great plan if she hadn't swept her foot across to stop the ball. The next instant she'd passed to Talia, with Kenneth on her left flank. Paulo marked Kenneth and Luca pressed forward to watch Talia. Mandy had followed up, and Kenneth punched a perfect pass toward the net. Mandy ran onto it and touched it softly to put it in.

Cody watched in a daze. Two goals in two touches. Paulo got the ball. No one said anything to Cody, which made it worse. Even Kenneth didn't make a joke. He felt totally pathetic. Paulo passed to him. He one-timed it back. He'd lost his confidence. Paulo gave it back again.

"I gotta tie my shoe," Paulo said. "Kill some time."

Mandy was on him like a shot. He was beginning to actively dislike her. And to think he'd taken a red card because Timothy insulted her.

Luca cut over and Cody was more than happy to send it to him. Luca held onto the ball until Paulo was ready.

"The shoe's operative," Paulo declared.

Luca passed it back. Paulo lazed to the right, surveying the scene. He caught Cody's eye. Cody knew what he wanted. Talia, Kenneth, and Mandy were in a straight line across. There was room behind them. Paulo faked an outside move. Cody brushed past Mandy. Paulo curled the ball over Kenneth's head, and it landed perfectly onto Cody's right foot. The net was wide open.

The next second he was skidding along the ground on his side. Mandy's slide tackle had taken his feet out from under him. Mandy got up and held out her hand.

"Good play," she said. "You almost had me there."

"I'm okay," he muttered. He tucked his foot under him and got up himself.

Mandy shrugged and took a few steps back. Cody backed away, too.

Paulo regained control and he passed to Cody inside. Cody kept his back to Mandy and considered his options. An elbow crushed into his ribs, as Mandy pushed to get to the ball. He instinctively threw his hip into her, which she ignored and pushed all the harder.

Cody was getting tired of this girl. He carried the ball toward his own goal to get some space. Mandy leaped by him on the right, cut across, and stripped him cleanly of the ball. All he could do was watch helplessly as she strolled down the field and scored — again.

"You weren't kidnapped by aliens who sucked your soccer skills out of your ears, by any chance?" Kenneth said to him.

Talia laughed. "Mandy takes things kinda seriously, if you haven't noticed. I'll tell her to mellow out."

"I'm . . . it's my fault . . . playing like garbage," he mumbled. He turned away. He didn't want Talia to see how angry he was.

He didn't mind playing with girls; and he knew there were tons of girls better than him. Somehow it felt like Mandy was making him look stupid on purpose, like she enjoyed it. She was grinning like crazy. It was a stupid pick-up soccer game, and she was playing like it was the World Cup final. He kept his head down and ran to re-trieve the ball.

They played for another half an hour, basically swapping goals. Talia came down with it, and when pressed by Luca, tried a cross in the middle to Kenneth. Cody ran over and headed the ball out of bounds.

"I'm too good a player to get that," Kenneth said.

He sat down. Luca came over and lay down on the field also.

"I'll get it," Cody said.

That was only fair. He'd headed it out. Cody jogged over. When he turned back, Talia was sitting.

"You guys quitting already?" Paulo said.

Paulo was like Cody. He could play forever.

"I'm not ashamed to quit," Kenneth said. "I'm really only ashamed of Luca."

"You should be ashamed for saying that," Luca said.

"What time is it?" Talia asked.

Paulo and Mandy sat too. Cody dribbled the ball back. He sat next to Kenneth.

"You don't have to go, do you?" Kenneth said to Talia.

"Not yet," Talia said. "Our moms decided we need to hang posters around town. Candice is organizing an anti-UPW meeting tomorrow night."

"I swear her head's gonna explode if they build the factory," Mandy said.

"I was reading about it — just websites and stuff," Paulo said. "UPW sounds like a dangerous company. I think your moms are right to protest. In Brazil, we're cutting down our rainforests just to raise cows to provide McDonald's with beef for their hamburgers. The rainforests clean the air for practically the entire planet, and those trees they're cutting down are huge, hundreds of years old. Not to mention cutting them down kills the habitat for insects and animals. My father took me to protests all the time — once we even got arrested." He flashed his toothy grin.

"You went to jail?" Talia said in amazement.

"We went to the police station and the cops asked my dad a bunch of questions. I didn't get put behind bars, although that would've been cool," Paulo grinned.

"Bro, that's so rebel. You're like a total renegade," Kenneth said.

"We were trying to protect the Amazon Climbing Salamander," Paulo laughed. "We weren't the toughest crowd in the world." Then he grew serious. "We have to stand up to these big companies. We can't let them cut down all the trees and kill whatever wildlife they want."

"I'm against what UPW wants to do, too," Mandy said. "Maybe my mom is a bit overboard — like way overboard — but she's right to warn people that UPW may end up polluting Lake Tawson."

"What can your moms do about it?" Kenneth said. "Isn't UPW going to build it anyway?"

"They can't yet," Mandy said. "UPW needs to get permission from the city. They need a permit from the four cities around Lake Tawson."

"They already have permission from two," Talia said.

Mandy leaned back on her hands. "Our city council is voting in a month, so there's still time. My mom thinks that if we get enough people to protest, the councillors will vote against UPW. No permit equals no factory."

"Where is this Lake Tawson?" Paulo said. "Is it far?"

"You've never seen it?" Talia said.

"Paulo's here for the summer with his family," Cody said. He just wanted to say something. He'd been sitting there like a statue.

"It's not far. We should show him," Talia said.

"I'm down for that," Paulo said.

"Do you have time?" Luca asked.

"We have until three thirty," Talia said.

Cody didn't want to go. It was such a private place for him. Besides, his mom and dad had grounded him. They'd said he could go to the park, but they didn't say anything about hanging out with friends at the lake. He tried to calculate how long they'd stayed at Auntie Beth's.

Kenneth ran to get his sweatshirt. "It's only eleven. Lots of time. Now listen up. I know you all want me to take charge because I'm your leader and you think I'm totally chill. Here's the plan. We go to Cody's and get his bike, and then Luca's for his. Then we go to my place. I've got enough bikes for the rest of you. We can ride to the Lake — and then everyone can tell stories about me, like why they want to be like me, and how everyone wants me to be their best friend and give them advice on everything. I guess we could also talk about why I'm the best soccer player ever . . . if there's time."

"We do that every day," Luca said. "Can't we do something else?"

"No," Kenneth said sharply.

Cody took a deep breath and followed them as they headed back to his house. He prayed Auntie Beth had made something awesome and his parents stayed there longer than usual.

They got the bikes and, before he knew it, Cody was climbing up and over a sand dune and heading across the beach. Seeing Lake Tawson again left him almost breathless. Last time he'd come was after his last treatment. He'd just been sick to his stomach, but he still begged his dad to bring him. He sat and sat, wrapped up in a blanket. No one was around, just him and his dad. He'd felt really calm and relaxed.

Cody couldn't remember the last time he'd felt like that. Life had somehow become more complicated once he'd gotten healthy.

A few people dotted the beach, families and a few couples, mostly at the far end near the main parking lot.

"What d'ya think?" Talia said to Paulo.

Paulo looked around. "Could this place be nicer? It's like a magazine cover."

"My mom told me even UPW admits they'll pollute the lake a little bit," Mandy said. "They're getting sued all over the place, but they don't care because they make more money than they ever pay out."

"What's the list of chemicals?" Talia said.

"Zinc and arsenic and copper . . . Can't remember them all," Mandy said.

"Manganese, selenium, and lead, too," Cody said. To their amazed looks he responded, "I did some research."

"I admit I do like a good manganese sandwich," Kenneth said.

"Do you come here much?" Paulo asked Cody.

Cody picked up some sand and let it run through his fingers. They were waiting for him to answer. Kenneth and Luca, with their faces friendly and open, Paulo, focused, excited, intense, Talia, smiling and unassuming, and Mandy, eyes wide open, staring intently, challenging him. But none of them had a clue how he felt about this place, how it had literally saved his life.

Cody looked out at the water. "I used to come here, mostly with my parents . . . well, all the time with them, when I didn't feel so good or got tired."

The boys grew quiet. They knew about his cancer. The girls didn't, obviously, although Mandy was looking at him kind of strangely.

"If you ask me, I say we do whatever it takes to stop UPW," Paulo said.

The breeze kicked up, the peaceful sound of the waves lapping up on the shore broken only by the far off shouts of kids hopping about in the lake.

"I like your fighting spirit, partner," Kenneth said, in a slow, Southern drawl. "But how are six measly kids gonna stop UPW? They have money, the mayor, and all the rich people in on it. And they've probably done this dozens of times before. What do we know?"

Talia kicked at the sand. "My mom drags me to protests, but no one listens. What's the point?"

"We know how to play soccer," Cody said quietly. An idea had come to him, a crazy idea, for sure, but it felt right — and he had to tell them.

Mandy let out an exasperated sigh. "Should we invite them to our games?"

"We can invite them to see us play," Cody said, "only not to our league games. We'll invite them here."

"We're playing here?" Talia said.

"Where else?" Cody said. In a weird way, he seemed to be talking to himself. "We play and play and play, right here, day after day, until people notice that we won't stop, we won't give up. People will start to ask why kids are playing soccer at Lake Tawson. They'll wonder why a bunch of kids love this place so much; and maybe . . . "

"A protest marathon game," Talia exclaimed. "I love it."

"All this time I thought Cody was so stupid and useless . . . and stupid," Kenneth said, "Then out of nowhere he comes up with the best idea ever invented."

"It's genius," Paulo said. "The newspapers and television people will go nuts. We'll get tons of free publicity. It'll go totally viral on social media."

"We can put up a website and a Facebook page with all the information about UPW, and why the council should vote no," Kenneth said.

"We can tweet every hour and put tons of pics on Instagram and Tumblr," Talia said.

"We'll get the rest of the team out," Luca said.

"We'll get our team, too," Talia said.

"I bet lots of kids will join us once they hear about it," Kenneth said.

"Don't forget to call Timothy," Paulo said.

"Who's he again?" Talia said.

"The big doofus who Cody decked," Kenneth said.

"We should start tomorrow," Mandy said. Her cheeks were flushed and her eyes danced about. "We have one of those big camping tarps . . . we can set it up by those trees and use it for breaks and to get out of the sun."

"We have a few coolers for water and food," Talia said.

"So do we," Kenneth said.

"How are we going to get the stuff here every day?" Luca asked.

Mandy's head drooped. "Are you forgetting we're dealing with my mom? She'll rent a fleet of trucks once she finds out about it."

Talia put an arm around Mandy's shoulders. "Our moms are so crazed they'll be setting up a buffet by the time we're done."

All at once they started laughing. It seemed so ridiculous.

"This is insane," Kenneth finally said. He was laughing so hard he was crying.

"We're really doing this?" Paulo asked.

"Definitely," Luca said.

"We can't do it tomorrow," Luca said. "We have a practice."

"We practice in the morning," Kenneth said. "We can meet later, say two o'clock, for the official kickoff."

A faraway look settled over Mandy. "Is this really going to work?"

Cody felt she was challenging him. He'd had enough of her for one day. "Soccer's the beautiful game, right?" he said.

"Yeah?" she said.

"Then the beautiful game is going to save a beautiful place."

"Guys, listen up," Kenneth said.

Practice was about to start. Trevor's truck had just pulled into the parking lot.

"We're planning to do something kinda nuts," he continued. "You all know about the company building the community centre, right? What you may not know is they're building a factory on Lake Tawson, and they're going to pollute it, and it could get so bad you'll never swim there again."

"My dad says that's all hype from the environmental crazies," William said.

"It's not," Paulo said. "The company — UPW — is being sued all over the world for polluting. We're going to hold a soccer game down at the beach to protest."

"We're calling it the Marathon Game," Kenneth said,

"and we'll have a website and a Facebook page up soon with lots of info about UPW."

"It's Mandy we're talking about," Luca said. "She probably has it up already."

"No pressure, guys, honest, but we could use you," Kenneth said. "The more we get out to play, the more people will notice and go to our website and find out what UPW really does."

"They're just a company trying to build a factory — and what about the community centre and the soccer fields?" Brandon said.

"They can keep their stupid community centre and fields," Paulo said.

"Easy for you to say. You're going home at the end of the summer. We live here," Brandon said.

Paulo snapped his head back.

Brandon coloured deeply. "I only meant that . . . since we live here, it's more important to us," Brandon said.

"The lake will be here longer than any of us," Paulo said.

"So . . . if you wanna come to the lake after practice, around two o'clock, we're going to kick it off," Kenneth said. "We want to play every day — me, Luca, Paulo, Cody . . ."

"Anyone else want to play?" Paulo jumped in.

"I'm up for it," Jordan said. "I can't come this afternoon, but another day, for sure."

Brandon clenched his jaw.

"I'll play, too," David said.

William spit some water on the ground. "Guys, I'm not saying I'm not on your side. I read some stuff, too. Only . . . my dad works for a company that might help build the water factory. It's . . . like . . . a really big deal for his company . . . and I don't think he'll let me play." His face darkened. "I even have to go to some UPW thing at the lake in a couple of weeks — a picnic or something."

Kenneth waved him off. "You don't have to apologize, bro. Totally get it."

"Not to mention the community centre and the fields," Brandon said.

Brandon seemed to be struggling to stop himself from saying more. Cody wondered what his own dad would say about the Marathon Game — or what Joel would say when he heard it was Cody's idea.

"That's what UPW does," Paulo said. "They try to bribe you with stuff, so they can dump their chemicals."

Brandon flushed and shrugged his shoulders.

"What about the Lions?" William said sharply.

Cody was taken aback. William was usually so easygoing.

"This isn't about the Lions," Kenneth said quickly.

"It is a little," William said. "We only have eleven guys on the team, and now you're doing this? I don't know."

"You don't know what?" Paulo said.

"Aren't you gonna get tired?" William said.

"We won't get that tired. We're just playing against each other," Luca said. "If you wanna play, great. If not, that's cool. We're just saying we'll be down there for the next month until the council votes on whether to let UPW build their factory."

"And it's the right thing to do," Paulo said.

"Not like they haven't built anything before. They know what they're doing," Brandon said.

Cody could tell Brandon was upset.

Paulo wasn't the type to back down. "Companies always lie to get their way," he said.

"My dad's not a liar," Brandon said.

Trevor blew his whistle and he jogged over.

"I assume you got my email yesterday," Trevor said. He didn't look at Cody, but Cody felt his gaze all the same. "The league had no sympathy with the fact we only have eleven players. The rules are clear: you must start a game with eleven players, no exceptions. Cody's red card means we forfeit our next game on Saturday."

A few boys groaned.

"We knew having only eleven would be a problem at some point," Trevor said. "So it happened. Not the best of circumstances, but such is life. We'll get over it and come out harder the next game, right?"

His call was met with gloomy silence.

"I totally, totally blew it, guys," Cody said. He felt sick to his stomach. "Totally on me. I guess I never thought about getting suspended and us having to forfeit the next game. Brutal of me." He found it hard to breathe.

"No one thinks you knocked Timothy down to make us forfeit — and we all know you two have had your differences," Trevor said. His tone was cold and direct. "Good defence, passing, triangularity are all essential aspects of learning to play soccer. But none of that will matter if you can't control your emotions. Hopefully, you've learned an incredibly important lesson. We tied a game we should have won — and now this. Selfish acts lose games. We lose one more and we're probably out of the playoffs."

The word *selfish* hit Cody like a punch in the gut.

And just like that he knew why he'd done it. He knew it with absolute certainty — and that hurt him way more than being called selfish. Sure, Timothy had bullied him and insulted Mandy. Those were the reasons he used to justify his actions. They weren't the real reason. Cody got angry at himself because he never could stand up to Timothy. He could never get up the nerve to dis guys when they dissed him, like at City Hall Square. Cody had gotten angry because he used to be terrified to come to practice — at least until Timothy and those guys quit. He'd almost quit the Lions because of the bullying. He would've quit if Kenneth hadn't convinced him to stay a little longer. It was just luck that Trevor took over the team.

The red card was his fault because he let Timothy make him feel bad about himself. He always thought Timothy was the most selfish soccer player he'd ever seen, never passing, always trying to be the centre of the action. But that wasn't true. Cody Dorsett was really the selfish player because he let his own feelings come before the team. He got himself kicked out and that let the Storm tie it up — and he'd caused the forfeit.

Trevor continued, "I know some of you are getting irritated with me and my attempts to teach you some aspects of a new style. The word 'triangularity' doesn't help much either. I'm not expecting you to play Spain's tiki-taka, one-touch passing game. I'm just trying to teach you how to play the modern game of soccer, with support, quick passes, and ball possession. You need to learn these things or you won't get better."

Their coach was obviously unhappy. Cody could hear it in his voice. Trevor was a former professional and he was fiercely competitive. It must be killing him that they might not make the playoffs.

"Give me William, Luca, and Kenneth in a triangle, with William and Luca five metres apart and Kenneth ten metres in front of them," Trevor said.

They lined up.

"Can everyone see the triangle?" Trevor asked.

They all nodded.

"I need a runner," Trevor said.

Cody's hand shot up. Trevor raised an eyebrow — and he pointed to the middle of the triangle. Cody was going to make up for that red card — and that meant working hard every second of every practice and every game.

"As you can see, the distance between William and Luca is smaller than the distance between either of them and Kenneth," Trevor said. "Cody doesn't have to run as far to

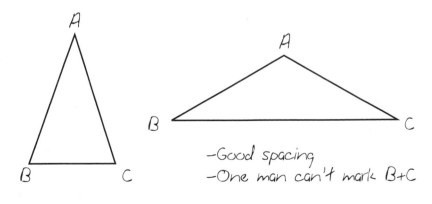

—Good spacing
—One man can't mark B+C

—B+C too close
—One man marks both

cover a pass from William to Luca, right? That's obvious."

Again, they nodded.

Trevor snapped a hard pass to William. "Cody, when I blow my whistle you charge William, and William you pass the ball to Luca when you think it's time. Luca, you pass to whomever you want."

TWEET!

Cody approached William, and when he was about two metres away, the ball shot right to Luca. Cody dashed to his left. Luca tried to slip the ball to Kenneth between Cody's feet, but Cody was able to drag a heel across and knock it away.

TWEET!

"So that short pass didn't work," Trevor said. "Why? Luca is so close to William that Cody only needed to take a step to the side and he could cover them both. Now let's try it with William passing to Kenneth."

They set up again. William sent it to Kenneth. Cody charged, but before he got close enough, Kenneth passed to Luca.

TWEET!

"Simple, right?" Trevor said. "Kenneth is far enough away that Cody can't stop the pass. Now imagine if after William passed to Kenneth, Luca had moved to his right to give Kenneth even more of an angle. Then, when Luca got the ball, what if William had taken a few steps back to open that passing lane — in other words, the triangle shifts to keep the passing lanes open. The ball carrier should always have two choices, and the best pass is the one that makes Cody run the farthest, while still being short enough to keep possession of the ball." He sketched two triangles on the board to show how the shifting triangle made it harder for the defender to get the ball.

"I think I get it," Cody said excitedly. "The players without the ball move to a spot where the ball carrier has a clear pass, either forward or back depending on what the defender does."

Trevor allowed himself a quick smile. "Give me groups of four. I'll play with the group of three. Now we practice, at top speed."

"You ready?" Luca said to Cody.

He knocked the ball to Kenneth. Cody took a step that way. Kenneth passed to Luca. Cody swerved to Luca, only Kenneth and William had shifted to give Luca two players to pass to. He chose Kenneth again. Cody had played keep-away a million times. It had never taken him this long to get the ball. After about twenty-five passes, he finally got a toe on the ball and knocked it to midfield.

"Good chasing," Trevor called out. "William, you switch up with Cody and let's keep going."

That sounded more like the usual Trevor. Cody would be forgiven, but only if he worked hard. He put the Marathon Game out of his mind. He was here to practice with the Lions!

8

"What do you mean by a protest?" Cody's dad said.

His stomach lurched at his father's tone. "I know you're working for UPW," Cody began. He reminded himself not to lose his temper. "It's just that . . . I don't agree — sorry. Lake Tawson, for me, well . . . it's where I went when I needed energy after a treatment. There's a chance UPW will pour chemicals into the lake, a real chance, maybe not one hundred per cent, but it's not zero, either."

"First off, I don't work for UPW. My company has contracted to do work for them. Second, safety standards are higher here than in other countries," his dad said.

"Can you tell me the lake won't be polluted? Can you guarantee it?" Cody said.

"Not fair. Nothing is guaranteed. I can only assume everyone involved will take every precaution . . . "

"Not good enough," Cody said harshly.

"Cody!" his mom said.

"Sorry, Dad," Cody said. But he wasn't, really. "I've read about this. I did some research on the Internet. There are tons of stories about UPW polluting water around the world."

"I agree there are issues around pollution — and that UPW projects have run into problems. It bothers me, too," his dad said. "Lots of us in the office are wondering if we should be working with UPW. But Joel and upper management don't care. They just want the money."

"I really wish you'd leave them — or start your own business. You could do it," Cody's mom said. "That Joel is impossible."

"And if you admit UPW is wrong, then you shouldn't do it," Cody said.

"I wish it was that simple," his dad said. "It means a job for me, and food on our table, and a roof over our heads."

"Let's not get over-dramatic, Sean," his mom said. "Food on the table?"

"Joel had been threatening to fire people for months before we got the UPW deal."

"You never told me that," she said.

His dad shrugged. "I didn't want to worry you."

Cody glanced at the clock. He was going to be late. "So can I go . . . ?"

His dad sighed. "I'm worried about Joel's reaction, to be honest. It's not going to look particularly good if . . . "

"I can't have an opinion?" Cody cut in.

"Of course you can," his dad said. He sounded almost

angry. "But it's easy to say UPW is bad. There's a lot of money at stake and jobs and a new community centre and . . . You have to admit, Cody, that it's possible UPW will never pollute Lake Tawson."

"Yeah, sure. It's possible."

"And that's all I'm saying. Unfortunately, I can't let my personal beliefs decide whether I work on this project or not. I can't. As for this marathon game — okay. I guess it's fine for now. Can't imagine Joel will ever hear about it."

"I have another concern, Cody," his mom said. "We can't risk you getting tired. This marathon game will exhaust you and the doctor said . . . "

Cody felt himself getting mad. "The doctor said I have to be careful about getting tired. I'm not tired, so I don't have to be careful. If I get tired, then . . . "

"Cody, you need to lower your voice," his dad said quietly.

Cody slumped in his chair and looked down at the table.

"You need to rest," his mom said. "Your friends understand . . . "

"That I had cancer and need my nap time?" Cody said sarcastically.

His mom threw her hands up in the air. Tears appeared in the corners of her eyes. "Do you enjoy making me upset? Sometimes I think you do."

Cody desperately wanted to leave. His mom was impossible to talk to when she got upset about his health. "How about I go today and we can see. I don't want to get tired, either. We can figure it out. Sure, if I'm totally exhausted or sick, I won't play."

"Totally exhausted won't be the test," his mom said tersely. "I'll be making the decision, thank you very much."

His dad took a sip of coffee and placed his mug on the table. Cody snuck a glance at the clock.

"I sorta gotta go," he said.

"When will you be home?" his mom asked.

"Don't know."

She slapped the table with her hand. "Unacceptable. I need a time — and you're keeping to it — not like this Saturday at City Hall."

"I told you. By the time we got food from the trucks the hour was gone," Cody said.

"Wear your watch from now on," she said.

"No one wears a watch," he groaned.

She held her wrist up.

"I don't mean you. Kids, I mean. They all have cell phones."

"Is this yet another attempt to get yourself a phone? I told you, not until high school. I don't want you to become another texting zombie," she said.

Cody had to laugh. That basically described every kid. "I'm willing to wait — even though I should get one. Then we could text each other every five minutes and you'll never have to worry about where I am."

"Don't tempt her," his dad said.

She tried not to laugh — unsuccessfully. "I'm trying, Cody. I want things to be normal. I do. But I'm not there yet. It's going to take a bit more time."

She'd said that before. For some reason, he felt this time she really meant it. And, that it was hard for her and she only worried because she loved him so much. He put his arms around her neck. He figured she needed a hug.

"We'll probably be done by five," he said.

She wiped her eyes after he let go. "Then I guess you should get going. Sean, can you give Cody a lift? When should we pick you up?"

"We're riding our bikes," Cody said. "I'm meeting up with some guys — Kenneth and Luca . . . and Paulo."

"And you're going to be playing soccer?" his dad said.

Cody nodded.

"Can I ask how that's a protest exactly?"

The way his dad said that made the Marathon Game sound a little dumb — and Cody worried whether he was right. "We figured it's what we're best at, playing soccer, and we're going to keep playing and playing until people pay attention. We're doing a Facebook page and a website, and the newspapers will be interested and . . . "

"Not sure anyone reads newspapers anymore," his dad laughed, "but good luck."

"Thanks. I . . . I should get going. See you later," Cody said.

He was more than happy to end this. He scurried out of the house, got his bike from the garage, and began to pedal to the lake.

A marathon soccer game? Were they crazy?

Four hours later, Cody wondered if his dad was absolutely right. Things started off great, and it was fun playing soccer on the beach. It was also exhausting. His mom would haul him home in a second if she saw him this tired. Paulo inched toward him. Everyone was moving at a snail's pace. Cody faked a pass to Kenneth and rolled the ball to Mandy. Paulo dropped to a knee. Luca had his hands on his knees. Mandy walked the ball forward. Talia was sitting down in goal.

"Just a thought, but maybe we should take a break before my legs fall off," Kenneth said.

"You're weak," Luca said, flopping to the ground.

"Running on the sand is brutal," Paulo said. He tumbled over.

Talia crawled over next to Kenneth.

"We need more players or we're gonna die," Kenneth said.

"I sent a ton of Facebook invitations," Talia said.

"Me too," Mandy said.

"Me three," Luca said. He lay down.

"We'll get people tomorrow," Kenneth said. "Think positive thoughts."

"Hope you're right. Until we do, we need some rules," Talia said. She sat on the sand with her knees to her chest and arms across her legs. "A marathon game can't mean we play for ten hours straight. How about we play for one hour and then take a twenty-minute break, and maybe thirty minutes for lunch?"

Cody thought that made sense.

"We gotta figure in time for soccer practices and games. And other stuff," Paulo said.

"What other stuff?" Mandy said.

"Things come up, family stuff, weekends. I mean — we could play from ten till two," Paulo said.

"Until we get more people maybe we should play twice a week," Luca said.

"We just got started," Mandy said.

"William mentioned something about a massive UPW picnic here in a couple of weeks," Kenneth said, "on a Saturday, I think, with prizes and music and games? My mom even wants to come. Maybe we shouldn't play then?"

"We just got started," Mandy repeated.

"I get the 'never say die' thing," Talia said. "But sometimes an idea sounds awesome, but then you actually do it and . . . well . . . it doesn't work so well."

"How often should we play?" Paulo said.

"Every day," Mandy said.

"We can't play every day," Kenneth said. "We have lives. I gotta leave soon for dinner. We got people coming over."

"I gotta get going soon, too," Luca said.

Cody was relieved to hear that others had to leave also. On the other hand, he was irritated that they were backing out of the Marathon Game so quickly. He was sure Mandy felt the same.

"Were you thinking we were gonna play seven days a week?" Talia said to Mandy.

"That was the idea, wasn't it?" Mandy said. "It's called the 'Marathon Game', not the 'Play Once In Awhile Game'."

"You got into the cause quick enough," Talia said. "You didn't even want to go to City Hall Square the other day, and now it's twenty-four seven."

Mandy threw a handful of sand to the side. "I was thinking about it — last night — and I guess I'm . . . I don't know . . . I want to do this — actually do it — at least do something. Better than waving signs in the air at people who don't care."

Kenneth dug a hole in the sand with his cleats. Paulo and Luca rolled the ball back and forth to each other. Cody looked out at the lake. The sun hit the water at a sharp angle, leaving shimmering, glittering triangles on the surface that got bigger and bigger farther away from shore. The air felt thick and warm, like a gentle soupy breeze. It was hard to imagine a nicer place.

"Not sure I have the energy for this," Kenneth said to break the silence.

"Maybe we got carried away?" Talia said.

They grew silent again. Cody could tell they wanted to quit. The idea of playing every day seemed fun yesterday — not so much now in the hot sun. Now it seemed more like hard work. Cody swallowed. His throat was really dry. He'd already drank all his water. He looked out at the lake again. These guys hardly knew him, and they wouldn't care about him coming here when he was sick. He owed it to the lake, however. He had to try. He swallowed again. For a horrible moment he thought he might cry.

"You know when you're playing soccer, say late in the second half, and after a long run you feel a bit dizzy and your chest hurts, and you just want to stop running?" Cody stopped. They were listening closely. "Of course, that's when the ball always comes to you. There's that moment when you have to decide whether you're going to go for it. When I was a kid I would quit running when I got tired . . . and then . . . well, I got sick and . . . it's different now. I push through it, and just ignore the fact that I can't breathe and my legs hurt and go after it."

Mandy and Talia wouldn't exactly know what he was talking about. They were soccer players, though. He had to hope they understood what he meant.

"You guys can play when you want. I get that you're busy. I don't have much to do this summer, other than the Lions. I just moved here. I don't know many people. Anyway, I'm gonna stay and play as much as I can. I'm serious." He could only imagine what his mom would say. "Even if I have to do it myself, I'm playing until the city council votes. I don't care if I don't change one person's mind. I'm doing it."

"What's the point if we don't change anyone's mind?" Talia said. "I'm sorry, Cody, but maybe the problem is people don't care. People come here once or twice in the summer. It's just a lake. We have lots of lakes."

"It's not just a lake. It's ... " Cody hesitated. They'd think he was crazy if he told them Lake Tawson saved his life.

"What's a Tawson anyway?" Kenneth said, yawning.

No one answered. Cody suddenly remembered the website he'd read before, about Percival and Charlotte. He told the story quickly.

"Are you making this up?" Talia gasped.

"It's for real," Cody said.

"And the letter really said 'hope is still glittering in my soul'?" Talia asked.

"Apparently, the letter is in a museum," Cody said.

"That's like the most romantic thing ever," Talia said.

"Positively dreamy," Kenneth said.

She stuck her tongue out at him.

"They buried Percival by the Lake and named it after him," Cody said. "There used to be a gravestone, but now no one knows where the grave really is."

"What happened to Charlotte?" Talia asked.

"According to the website, her dad forced her to marry another boy, but she died before the wedding — it said of a broken heart," Cody said.

"Come on, guys. Admit it. That's romantic," Talia said. "Mandy, a little support on this please."

"I guess there's a bit of romance," she said.

Kenneth leaned back on his hands. "Just what I wanted

to do with the rest of my summer — seven days a week playing soccer on the shores of Lake Tawson." He turned to Cody. "Why'd you have to say 'hope is still glittering in my soul'? Now I can't give up — ever. You've ruined summer. Great work, bro."

Cody smiled uneasily.

Luca struggled to his knees. "I'm in — but when I die from exhaustion could you bury me over there beneath those trees, beside Percival?"

"They don't know where he's buried," Paulo said.

"I'm pretty good with dead things. He's right there." Luca pointed to the forest near the path that led up to the small parking lot.

"Kinda creepy, but we'll take your word for it," Kenneth said. "I say we bury Luca now. May as well get it over with. Problem is we don't have a shovel."

"I have a plastic mini-shovel at home. I used to bring it here to play on the beach when I was a kid. And the best part: it's neon pink," Talia said.

Kenneth's head whipped around. "You have a neon pink shovel and you didn't bring it?"

"Selfish," Luca said.

Paulo sprung to his feet. "We should keep score from now on. Winner gets the shovel."

"Are you willing to sacrifice Pinky to save Lake Tawson?" Kenneth asked Talia.

"Won't have to," Talia said. "No way you three hooligans can beat me, Paulo, and Luca."

Kenneth's face twisted in disgust. "Puh-lease. You may as well give us Pinky now."

"Pinky ain't goin' nowhere," Talia said.

"Pink-y, Pink-y, Pink-y," Luca chanted.

Cody couldn't stand it. "Are you guys actually gonna play?"

Paulo offered a lopsided grin and booted the ball down the beach. "You guys are so sad and pathetic we'll even let you kick off."

"You're only saying that because we're sad and pathetic," Kenneth said.

Paulo looked around awkwardly. "Yeah. Kinda."

"Fine. We'll take the ball," Kenneth said, "and thanks for the most awesome team name ever."

"Which is?" Luca said.

"The Sad and Pathetic Football Club," Kenneth said. "Me, Cody, and Mandy. And Percival's our coach."

"A very fitting name," Talia said.

"At least we have one," Kenneth shot back.

"We've got a name," Luca said.

They waited.

Luca burst out laughing. "But it's none of your beeswax."

"No — that's it. But it's not beeswax," Talia said. "It's the Mighty Bees — and Charlotte's totally our coach."

"Actually, I need to go to the washroom," Luca said. "Right now, it's the Mighty Pees."

Kenneth pressed his knees together and nodded vigorously toward the forest. "Unfortunately, you might need to change your name to the Mighty Poos. I had chili for lunch."

Luca wrapped his hands against his stomach. "I maybe had two tuna sandwiches for lunch. Change the name to the Mighty Poo Poos to include both of us."

"That tree looks interesting," Kenneth said.

"Good thinking," Paulo said.

"The boy gross-factor is getting way too high," Talia said.

"Sorry for what I'm about to say, but I might need to combine the two names," Kenneth said, bulging his eyes out.

"Okay, so the name is the Mighty Poo Poos and Pee Pees Football Club," Luca said.

"It totally is not," Talia said. She looked up to the sky. "Please, someone make boys normal. Please!"

"You're talking about Luca, right?" Kenneth whispered to Talia.

"Our name is the Mighty Charlotte Stompin' Sad and Pathetic Crushers," Talia declared.

Luca mouthed the name to himself. "The McStompers it is," he said. He held his hand to his heart. "I give you the team anthem:

WE'RE THE MCSTOMPERS, YES WE BE,

GOTTA PEE BEHIND THAT TREE,

SAD AND PATHETIC ARE VERY WIMPY,

AND WORSE THAN THAT THEY'RE KINDA STINKY.

"All together now, people," Kenneth declared, his arms and legs pumping like the leader of a marching band.

The boys began to sing Luca's ridiculous rhyme as they marched to the forest. All the while, Cody's head was whirling. The words had poured out of him, and he still couldn't believe they'd decided to play. He walked after them, nervously. What were they really thinking?

Cody punched the ball to Brandon wide right in a long high arc. Brandon paid no attention as it sailed out of bounds. He walked over to William, Jacob, Austin, and Ryan.

This practice wasn't going right, and not just because the guys who played in the Marathon Game that morning seemed tired, which wasn't surprising since it was the fourth straight day they'd played. It wasn't right because the guys weren't joking around like usual. Whenever there was a whistle or a break between drills, guys would talk to each other in whispers.

No one looked happy. And Cody knew the Marathon Game was why.

Cody had spent most of the practice struggling to find the courage to say something about it. It was one thing to speak up at the beach in front of five people — but in front of the entire team? They wouldn't listen to him. He looked around. Paulo was talking to Trevor. Kenneth, Luca, and David were huddled near centre.

He figured he could start with those three guys.

"Not the greatest practice ever," Cody offered.

Kenneth opened his eyes and shrugged.

"I think we sorta don't have a ton of energy . . . some of us . . . like me," Cody said.

"Maybe," Luca said.

Cody forced himself to keep going. "Yeah . . . I guess . . . and maybe some guys — the guys who aren't Marathon Gamers — maybe they're not exactly happy with what Paulo posted on Facebook last night?"

"What did he post?" David asked.

"Paulo wrote that anyone who didn't come to the beach was being a UPW slave and a chicken, and they didn't have the right to go to the beach anymore," Luca said uneasily.

"Okay . . . " David said.

"And I think they're not exactly happy with us because they figure we think the same way," Cody said in a rush to get it all out.

"Well . . . they decided not to play," Kenneth said.

Trevor's whistle blew. "Take a knee around me, lads. I want to go over a few things before I let you go," he said.

Cody was happy to sit. His legs were dead.

"First off, practice was a bit ragged," Trevor said. "Some of you weren't going full out. I know you guys are a bit bummed out about the default. Let it go. That's in the past. We have to look ahead to our next game against the Panthers. Every game is vitally important now, and . . . "

"Has nothing to do with the default," Brandon said.

Cody noticed that Brandon and Jordan weren't together. They were best friends, practically inseparable. Jordan had begun to play at the lake with them, along with David.

Trevor rubbed his chin with his hand. "What's up?"

Brandon shrugged. "Ask the Marathon Gamers," he said.

Trevor's eyes widened. "Not sure I follow."

Brandon kept his gaze to the ground.

Trevor took a knee as well. "I've been on too many teams to count. The teams that won did so because they stuck together. They played for each other. Those that lost — you can guess why. So I'm asking again, what's up?" His voice had an edge to it.

Cody wanted to answer desperately. He couldn't bring himself to speak. The other guys would turn on him.

"I don't have a problem with the Marathon Game," William said, "only it's not fair to have it thrown in our faces and for us to be called cowards and slaves."

"I didn't say that," Paulo said.

"Huh?" Brandon said. "Now you're telling me I can't read?"

"I wrote that kids should come if they want to stop UPW from polluting the lake," Paulo said hotly.

"You wrote if we didn't play we were UPW slaves and cowards and . . . "

Trevor cut Brandon off. "Can someone tell me what's actually going on?"

Cody had to say something. No one was answering Trevor directly. "It's what we're calling the Marathon Game," Cody said. "Some of us, well, me, Luca, Paulo, and

Cody, and then Jordan and David, we've started to play soccer to protest against UPW and the factory it wants to build on Lake Tawson."

"And it's called the Marathon Game because . . . ?" Trevor's voice faded.

"We play all day," Luca said.

"We take breaks," Paulo said.

"Not that many, obviously," William said. "You guys walked the entire practice."

"You try playing soccer all morning and then come to practice," Paulo said, his eyes flashing angrily.

"So the Marathon Game is more important than the team?" Austin asked.

Paulo was obviously shocked to hear that from Austin. He was the quietest kid on the team. "No . . . obviously . . . No . . . Of course not. Lake Tawson is important . . . "

"Why's it more important that the Lions?" Brandon said. "Why do you care so much? You don't even live here."

"So you want me to go back to the jungle, too?" Paulo said, eyes flashing.

"That's so wrong!" Brandon thundered. "All I meant was you're going home in a couple of months and you act like you can tell us what's important and what's not. I don't tell you what to do in Brazil. I'm not racist because I have an opinion about Lake Tawson and the community centre."

Paulo shrugged and looked down. He began to pull chunks of grass out of the ground.

"Maybe you guys can tone it down on practice days, and for sure don't play before a game?" Trevor said. "I'm not expressing an opinion about this Marathon Game or Lake

Tawson. That's a personal matter. This team is my concern, however. A team divided will never win. Never! We need to separate the personal stuff from the Lions; otherwise, we're wasting our time. Paulo and Brandon, I need you to shake hands. You're teammates, and UPW shouldn't change that."

"I can have an opinion, too," Paulo said. "Lake Tawson doesn't belong only to the people who live close to it. Everyone on the planet should care — because we live on the same freakin' planet."

"So everyone has to do what you tell them?" Brandon yelled.

"Yeah, right. Like that's what I said," Paulo answered.

"Boys, that's enough!" Trevor said.

"You tell him that . . ."

"Brandon! That's enough," Trevor said. Cody had never seen Trevor get this angry. "Practice is over. Paulo and Brandon, stay here. We need to talk." He took Brandon and Paulo off to the side.

The guys who didn't play in the Marathon Game left in a pack.

"That wasn't too good," Luca said.

"There was nothing good about that," Kenneth said.

"Paulo didn't mean those guys are slaves and cowards," Cody said. "You know how things come across sometimes online." Paulo had always been the best teammate, a total team player, and one of the nicest kids Cody had ever met.

"But he wrote it," Kenneth said.

"Like I said, maybe it come across a bit harsh . . ." Cody began.

"I agree. Only . . ." Kenneth threw his arms up in the

air. "I don't know. Why don't they come and play — even once? Their parents shouldn't be telling them what to do. They should make up their own minds — or at least like our Facebook page."

"Would you play if your mom and dad said you couldn't?" Cody said to Kenneth.

"I would once — or I'd send a text while they were playing saying sorry I can't come," Kenneth said.

They headed to the sidelines.

Kenneth's dad waved his hand. "Let's get going, boys. Nice practice. So what's Trevor going on about over there?" he said.

Trevor was still talking to Brandon and Paulo.

"Dunno," Kenneth said. "I think they're going over some new plays." He flashed a grin at Cody and Luca. "Is it okay to drop us off at the lake? We wanna meet up with some people and play a bit more."

His father cocked his head. "Isn't that overdoing it a wee bit? You were there this morning."

"Well . . . it's sorta called the Marathon Game for a reason," Kenneth said.

Mandy had made them promise to come back after practice. To be honest Cody would've been happier to go home. His mom was going to be all over him for playing too much. Truth was he was finding it tough to keep his energy up, and the other Marathon Gamers were dragging their butts lately, too. This practice was proof of that.

"All right. Get in the car. I'll take you. I assume you boys need a lift?" he said to Luca and Cody.

"Not Luca," Kenneth said. "He likes to walk."

"I think I'd prefer to drive just Luca and Cody," Kenneth's dad said drily. "It'll be a lot quieter." He pressed the fob and the doors clicked open. Cody took a seat. He wondered what he'd do if his dad told him he couldn't go to the Marathon Game. Would he lie and play anyway or send texts and support them in some other way?

Trevor was holding his arms wide apart and he was shaking his hands in the air. Paulo and Brandon stood in front of him, arms crossed. Cody thought about what Trevor had said. Half a team can't win. Everyone needs to be on board. They needed to do something to fix this — and fast. Otherwise, the Lions could kiss their playoff chances goodbye.

The boys kept their thoughts to themselves during the drive over; even Kenneth was quiet for the most part.

"I can pick you guys up later," Kenneth's dad said as they piled out of the van.

"We won't be playing too long," Kenneth said. "Maybe until seven?"

His dad nodded and drove off.

Luca let out a loud groan. "Can we change the name to the Marathon Sleep? I'm trashed."

"I'm a little tired, too," Cody said.

Actually, he was totally wiped out. The car ride had stolen whatever energy he had left.

"Kids today are pathetic," Kenneth said. "All you do is watch YouTube, play video games, and text. You disgust me. Now give me a pillow. I can't keep my eyes open."

They headed down the path to the beach.

"I guess we promised," Cody said. The truth was he didn't want to let Mandy down.

"We also made a promise to our teammates," Luca said. "I kept waiting for my energy to come back at practice — but nothing. I was like a zombie."

"Let's not start insulting zombies now," Kenneth said.

"Maybe Trevor has a point," Cody said. "We shouldn't be playing before a practice or a game."

"I nominate Cody for telling Mandy," Kenneth said.

"I guess I've lived long enough," Cody said.

To his surprise, Kenneth and Luca laughed.

"It's been good knowing you," Luca said.

"So . . . can I have your soccer ball?" Kenneth asked.

"As long as you can give it a good home," Cody said.

Luca rolled his neck. "That still doesn't solve the problem with the team," he said. He kicked aside a branch that had fallen across the path.

"I don't think Paulo meant to dis the guys," Cody said.

"I'm not sure what he meant," Kenneth said. "Cowards and slaves — that's intense stuff."

"But he didn't mean the guys on the team," Cody said.

"And Brandon didn't call him . . . well, I don't want to say it," Luca said.

"It's all messed," Cody said.

"We just got rid of Timothy and those jerks and now we're divided into two teams again?" Luca moaned.

His question went unanswered. Cody spotted the sand dune up ahead. He took a deep breath. Even the thought of climbing the dune made him tired. He had to talk to Mandy. He owed it to the Lions — and to himself.

Cody groaned as he bent to tie his shoes. His entire body hurt.

"Too much soccer, Dorsett," he said.

He'd come home the night before after seven thirty, in time for a wicked lecture from his mom about running himself ragged. They'd had a big fight about him playing today. She'd only let him go after he'd promised to come home by four o'clock. That was going to be totally awkward. The teams would be uneven. He walked down the stairs.

WE'RE THE MCSTOMPERS, YES WE BE,

WE GOTTA PEE BEHIND THAT TREE . . .

He needed to get that stupid song out of his head. Of course, Kenneth and Luca kept adding verses. Talia had made up a few good ones, too. They'd even started to think of a song for the Sad and Pathetic Football Club. How did it go?

I'M SAD,

HE'S PATHETIC,

PUT IT TOGETHER,

WE'RE COPACETIC.

He hadn't known what copacetic meant and didn't want to sound stupid, so he'd just joined in. He'd looked it up when he got home — it meant everything worked well, things were cool, things were all right. That wasn't really true. Things weren't copacetic. Paulo didn't want to talk about his Facebook post after practice at the beach. Cody agreed with Kenneth that Brandon would never say anything racist.

"I have smoked-meat sandwiches and I cut up some fruit, too," his mom said.

He hopped down the last few stairs. "Peanut butter would've been fine, and no one asked for fruit."

"Please. You're playing so much. It's important to eat to keep the energy up."

They left and got into the car.

"Where do you eat?" she said.

"Mandy's mom brings a big camping tarp and Talia's mom brings coolers with ice and water."

"Who's Mandy and Talia?"

His mom could ask the weirdest questions. "Just two girls playing in the Marathon Game."

"How'd you meet them?"

"They played soccer with Kenneth and Luca and . . ." He figured that was enough info.

Before long they pulled into the parking lot.

"I haven't been here in so long," she said. She pulled the keys from the ignition. Her face darkened.

"That's over now, Mom. I'm here to play soccer," Cody said.

His mom dabbed the corner of her eyes with a tissue. "You're right, dear. Being here brings back a lot of difficult memories. Sometimes you were so weak Daddy had to carry you, remember? He'd set you up in a chair and wrap you in a blanket. With your cap on, all we could see were your eyes and nose sticking out. You were like a little sausage."

No stopping the tears now. She twisted in her seat and gave him a hug. He could only pray no one came by. He reached for the door handle.

"Okay, little sausage, let's go," she laughed.

"Go . . . ?"

"I want to see where you're playing."

"It's the beach. You've seen it a thousand times."

"Let's make it a thousand-and-one."

Cody got out and his mom did, too. Why couldn't she leave him alone?

"I also wanted to tell you how proud I am that you've decided to get involved like this and make such a commitment," she said. "It's scary for kids, I think, this crazy world, with global warming, pollution, and the destruction of so much of the environment. It's your futures we're talking about, and I love that you're interested. Most kids don't care about anything but their Facebook page and video games."

Cody hadn't expected that. "The other kids deserve the credit," he said. "They organized things. Mandy did the online stuff."

"I'm proud of you, regardless," she said. "I know it's difficult with Daddy and his work. But you should do what your conscience tells you. That's what your dad and I want." She frowned. "When you're older and there are bills to pay, you have to make difficult choices."

What if they won and UPW didn't build the factory? Would his dad lose his job? What would his family do then?

They continued along the path that led to the beach.

"You're not feeling run down or tired, are you?" she said.

"I feel fine, Mom," Cody said.

"I see some serious bags under those eyes," his mom said. "Maybe I'll swing by at two o'clock and you can ... "

"I feel great, Mom, never better. I don't need to go to bed at two o'clock."

"I didn't say you had to go to bed."

"Can I stay up until two thirty, then?"

"If you want to be sarcastic we can turn around and go home right now," she said.

Cody gritted his teeth and nodded. "I told you that we stop for lunch and take lots of breaks. How about four o'clock, like we agreed?" he said in an even tone.

"Okay. Good. I'm just looking out for you, honey. Kids don't always take care of themselves. Anyway, tell me, this Mandy, who is she again? Where does she go to school?"

"I don't really know her, Mom." He walked ahead. Every time he mentioned a girl his mom acted like they were about to get married. "It's just over this sand dune," he called back.

He stopped at the top of the dune. Mandy and Candice had strung up the camping tarp already. Candice came out from under the tarp and waved.

"And who do we have here?" she said as they walked up. She wore black yoga pants, white sneakers, and a baseball cap, and she had big sunglasses with red rims.

"That's Cody," Mandy said.

"Oh, so this is Cody. Very nice to meet you. And is this your mom?"

"I'm Cheryl."

"Wonderful to meet you. I'm Candice. Hey, Mandy, came say hi to Cody's mom." Candice giggled and gave Cody's mom a big hug. "Mandy and Cody — they sound so cute together." She let out a peal of laughter. "Cheryl, I can see him in your face. You have the exact same eyes, for sure. Don't you think, Mandy?'

Mandy shrugged.

"Cody, were you at City Hall Square the other day?" Candice asked. "Cheryl, you wouldn't believe what the police did to us. We were protesting peacefully, and they kicked us off City Hall Square, which is supposed to be for the people, no? UPW has the police totally paid off — along with city council, no doubt."

"I can't believe the police would take money from . . . "

Candice cut his mom off. "Trust me. UPW's totally corrupt. Their chemicals are killing our children. But we'll stop them. Right, Mandy?"

Mandy shrugged again.

"We got here a little early to set up the tarp for the kids," Candice said. "We used this tarp a lot when we went camping." Her lips pressed together tightly, as if something had begun to bother her. "It gets hot on the beach, and they need some shade," she continued, her voice a little strained. "It's easy enough to take down. I'll come and get it tonight. We brought some water and food, too."

"We have some sandwiches and fruit," Cheryl said.

Cody held up his backpack.

"Excellent!" Candice said, and she clapped her hands. "Can you two kids be dears and run to the car and bring down the other cooler, and I think I left a water jug, too. The keys for the van are in my purse."

Mandy took the keys. Cody's mouth went dry. Walk all the way to the parking lot and back with Mandy, just the two of them? What would they talk about? Mandy headed to the path.

"Go on," Candice said. "Mandy needs a big, strong man like you to help."

His mom had that half-crazed smile she always got whenever the topic of girls came up, like him getting a cooler from a van was a big romantic thing. He trudged

107

after Mandy. Typically, she was booting it and was over the sand dune already. He didn't want to look like a slow-poke, so he ran to catch up — and very nearly ran into her.

"Sorry, thought you were way ahead," he said, and then caught himself. Her eyes were a little puffy. "Mandy? You okay?"

"I'm fine," she said.

They set off, side-by-side. Cody figured he should say something. They couldn't walk there and back and not say a word to each other.

"Do you guys camp a lot?"

She gave him a sideways glance. "Not anymore."

"How come?"

"Parents got divorced," she snapped.

"Sorry." He forged ahead. He'd tried to be nice, but if she was going to treat him like that, forget it.

Mandy grabbed his wrist to hold him up. Her smile faded quickly. "I give everyone a hard time, so don't take it personally. My mom and I had a huge fight before you came and . . . I guess it carried on in my head. I'm sorry."

Cody relaxed his shoulders and let out a breath. "Me and my mom sorta got into a fight on the way over, too."

"What about?"

"She's a bit overprotective, and that's why she drove me here and then came down to the beach, to check things out and meet you guys. It bugs me. She's maybe gotten better since . . . She's gotten better, but it just bugs me."

Mandy cleared her throat and her eyes got glossy. "My brother had cancer, too," she said softly.

Cody closed his eyes for a moment. The boys must have

108

told. "That's too bad," he said, and then added, "how did you know?"

She flushed. "After what Gavin went through, I can tell, with your hair and all. What kind did you have?"

"It was a lump in my leg. I was lucky and it didn't spread. They took it out in a surgery and then they did radiation and chemotherapy to make sure all the cancer is dead."

"Is it?"

He held his arms out. "I have to wait five years. After that I'm cured."

She took a moment. "Your mom is just worried about you. That's what moms do," she said.

"I know. I just wish she'd leave me alone a bit more. She's way better now, trust me. She was insane when I had cancer. If I sneezed, she'd call an ambulance."

Mandy tilted her head.

"Okay, maybe that's an exaggeration, but not by much," Cody said.

They began walking again. "My mom was like that with Gavin, obsessed with his health, like what he ate and when he went to sleep. She made him go on these crazy diets, tons of fruits and vegetables. She even made sure his toenails were cut right. It was weird, and it drove Gavin nuts, but he never complained. He told me it was Mom's way of trying to control the cancer. I acted like a brat because I was so scared . . . " She wiped her eyes. "Can I ask you a question — about cancer?"

He didn't really want to talk about it, but he couldn't exactly say no. "Yeah, sure. What about?"

"What's it like?" she said. "Gavin wouldn't talk about it with me."

Cody kicked at a branch. The leaves bounced up and fluttered in the air. He'd never talked about that with anyone. He had to think about it first. "You feel like there's an alien in your body," he said finally. "For some reason I couldn't stop seeing this grey, spongy thing in my leg, all leaky and gross. Doesn't make sense, and the doctor showed me pictures of what a tumour looks like, but it didn't help. I'd even dream about it. I'd see this grey thing in my leg, and it would work itself up my body and come out my throat and wrap around my neck, and I'd wake up screaming and choking . . . "

He had to stop. For a second he felt it again.

Mandy put a hand on Cody's shoulder. "I bet your mom was there to put you back to sleep," she said.

He took a deep breath. "I guess that's what moms do — that and embarrass their kids," he joked.

She didn't laugh. "I'm just happy you're okay."

He kicked at another branch, so she couldn't see him blush. "How's Gavin doing?"

Mandy crossed her arms and rocked on her heels. "He had leukemia, which is cancer of the blood. He died two years ago."

Cody's head began to spin. "Oh, I . . . I'm . . . I didn't know . . . "

"My mom lost it — like — she couldn't deal with it, and my dad couldn't deal with her, and they got divorced — about six months ago. That happens a lot, parents splitting up after their kid dies, at least that's what my counselor told me. My parents make me go to a woman to talk about Gavin and the divorce. It's dumb." She shrugged.

"Is she nice?"

"I guess."

"Sorry about your parents."

Mandy had a faraway look in her eyes. "Everyone loved Gavin, especially my mom. When he died, I kinda think she died, too, on the inside."

"Your mom? She has lots of energy."

"You don't really know her. In front of people, she's always like that, laughing or organizing stuff. I think she acts like that to keep her mind off Gavin, because every night she's totally quiet, doesn't talk to me, and just goes to bed. Half the time I think she cries herself to sleep. She has this weird habit of talking about Gavin like he's still here. Before you came she was telling me how Gavin would've loved to play soccer on the beach with us. And he would've brought a hundred friends — unlike me who only has Talia . . . "

Mandy let out a sob. Cody felt helpless. She was probably only telling him this because he'd had cancer. So he figured the best way to make her feel better was to talk about that.

"Remember when I said I used to come to Lake Tawson with my parents?" Cody began. "Well, I'd come here when I was sick, really sick. Sometimes I'd feel so gross I would want to give up, just to make the sick feeling go away, cause you get tired of being so sick. They'd bring me down and put me in a chair and wrap me in a blanket because it was cold, especially with the wind. I wouldn't want to leave — the fresh air, the sound of the waves, the forest — it made me want to stay alive, to not give up. Maybe this place will do the same thing for you and your mom?"

"That's a nice story," Mandy said. "I don't think so, but I'm glad you told me. Makes sense why you want to save the lake so bad."

"Well . . . there's more to it, I think," Cody said. "I guess because I used to come here when I was sick I thought about my fight with cancer. Because the strange thing about it is you don't really fight, not like in a soccer game where you win by playing harder than the other team. Cancer is too strong to fight like that. It's like a brick wall. When I got really, really sick and tired, I stopped fighting, couldn't anymore. All I could do was accept that I was sick and not give in. I ignored everything and kept going. I got lucky and the cancer quit before me. That's how I got the idea for the Marathon Game. We don't give in to UPW and hope they quit first."

"I didn't think you were a quitter," Mandy said.

"No more than you."

"I'm just a troublemaker."

"That's what we need," Cody laughed. "We need a whole bunch of troublemakers."

"We should hurry," Mandy said. "Our moms will have nervous breakdowns if we're not back soon — at least yours will. Mine will still be talking."

They began to run up the path.

"You don't think you can beat me, do you?" Mandy said.

"Kinda."

They sprinted full out. Cody was used to winning races. Mandy matched him stride-for-stride. They got to the entrance together.

"Which van is it?" Cody said, puffing hard after their run.

Mandy raised her eyebrows. He laughed. There was only one van. The only other car was his mom's.

"I sometimes say stupid things to be funny," he said.

She giggled at that, which made him feel better.

"Stupid that we still have a van since it's just Mom and me," Mandy said. "She won't sell it."

"Because of Gavin?"

Mandy pressed the button and the trunk popped open. "She says it's in case we need the space — which we never do."

"Sorry for asking that," Cody said.

"You don't have to say sorry — not your fault."

"I didn't mean that, only . . . "

"I was sorta joking, Cody."

He let his arms flop to his sides. "I'm always doing that. Pathetic."

"It is," Mandy said, "but cute, too." She pulled the cooler out.

He didn't know how to take that. Was she making fun of him? What was cute about it? They were the same age, so why treat him like a little kid? For once he needed to stop taking people so seriously. It was getting embarrassing, and he was sure it was a joke among the other kids.

"Earth to Cody?" Mandy said. She held a handle out.

"Sorry," he said.

"You really gotta get that *sorry* habit under control," she said.

"Sorry."

"Cody!"

"I was sorta joking?"

That felt good. He'd made the joke without even thinking about it. It just came out.

Mandy looked shocked. "Cody — that was actually funny. I'm proud of you. We'll make a comedian out of you yet." She tugged on the cooler. "C'mon."

He grabbed the other handle and together they set off down the path.

The whistle blew. The referee backed away from the side-line for the throw in.

"Focus, Lions," Kenneth said, clapping his hands a few times.

"Put the ball on my foot," Brandon snapped.

Kenneth's pass to Brandon had been a touch too hard and the ball had rolled out of bounds. A Panthers mid-fielder held the ball over his head. Luca ran to mark him.

"I got him," Brandon said. "You get that guy."

"Fine. Mark him if you like him so much," Luca scowled.

Brandon scowled at Luca.

"Heads up for the throw in, defence," Paulo hollered between cupped hands.

"Heads up for the throw in, forwards," Jacob hollered back.

"Let's go, guys. We're winning 4–0," Cody said to Brandon and Luca.

They both shrugged. Cody clenched his fists — and went to mark a defender. They were winning, and he'd never enjoyed a game less. The Lions had been dissing each other from the first whistle.

The throw in went to the Panthers right back. He squared the ball inside.

"I got him," Cody said.

Ryan also charged up.

The defender punched the ball between them.

Cody hopped up and slammed his feet to the ground.

"I had him," Cody said. Trevor had been on them about that in practice. Two guys pressure the ball carrier together only if they can trap him and prevent a pass.

"Sorry, Mister Superstar," Ryan said.

"All I meant was . . . "

Ryan ran off before Cody could finish.

The Panthers midfielder curled slowly toward his right. Kenneth pressed forward, knees bent low, hands to the sides, watching warily.

"Get him!" Brandon cried.

He flew over and knocked the ball away with a fierce slide tackle. Ryan corralled the bouncing ball. Cody came hustling back.

"Quick pass," Cody said. He waved at Paulo to spread out.

Ryan fed it back to William in the middle of the field, about five metres from the top of the box.

"Look for the opening," Cody said. "Me and Paulo had a fast break."

"Worry about your own play," Brandon said to Cody.

"Why do we even bother playing? You guys can do it all by yourselves," Ryan said.

William dribbled to his right and then rolled the ball to Austin camped out by the right sideline.

"What's up with you guys, anyway?" Kenneth muttered. He began to jog away.

"I'm tired of you guys acting like you're all professionals because you play soccer on some beach," Brandon said. "Gets irritating after a while."

Paulo edged over. "Not our fault we got the skills," Paulo said, his eyes flashing darkly.

"Whatever," Brandon said. "You're so perfect, obviously. You never make a mistake. And everyone has to do what you tell them. Sorry — forgot."

Ryan took a pass from Austin. He took two steps forward and passed it back. Austin in turn gave the ball to Jacob. Kenneth presented himself for a pass. Jacob gave it to William.

"Let's play soccer, Lions!" Kenneth yelled. He clapped his hands and stomped a foot on the ground.

"What do you think we're doing?" Jacob said.

William returned the ball to him, and again Jacob sent it wide right to Austin.

"I think you're making dumb passes," Kenneth said angrily.

"Let's get one more and forget about all this," Cody pleaded. The fighting was making him queasy.

Jordan and Ryan scooted to the right in support.

"We already agreed that it's no big deal if you play in the

Marathon Game," Kenneth said to Brandon. "So what's your point, already?"

"Guys, we're in the middle of a game," Cody said.

Most of the guys had stopped running. The Panthers had basically given up and weren't putting too much pressure on the ball, fortunately.

"Yeah, and hopefully it'll be done soon," Brandon said. He took a few steps forward and waved a hand for the ball.

Austin gave it to Ryan, and he chipped the ball over Kenneth's head to Brandon. Paulo leapt up and tried to intercept the ball. It grazed his toe and deflected to the left.

The turnover seemed to energize the Panthers all of a sudden. The three forwards poured into the Lions end, along with all three midfielders.

"Hog the ball much?" Brandon yelled over his shoulder at Paulo, as he raced to get back.

"Shut . . . " Paulo kicked his toe into the ground and growled. He sidestepped toward the middle of the field.

"Having fun yet?" Jordan muttered to Cody. He drifted to the right.

The Lions back line pressed up as one and the Panthers ball carrier had to slow down to prevent his teammates from going offside.

"Go, Lions!"

Brandon had snuck behind and stripped the Panthers player of the ball, and the Lions parents gave him a big cheer. Brandon whirled and headed up field.

"I'm going wide left," Cody called out to Paulo. He wanted to stretch the defence, although he wondered if

Brandon would pass to any of the Marathon Gamers.

The Panthers centre left midfielder got back to pressure. With so many Panthers still trapped, Brandon couldn't play the ball to any of the Lions defenders. He had no choice but to pass to Kenneth. Paulo cut right sharply and Kenneth rewarded Paulo's quick thinking with a sharp pass. Paulo took it without slowing and cut back left. The four Panthers defenders back-pedalled frantically.

Cody took a few steps inside and Paulo passed him the ball. A defender charged him. Cody heard cleats pounding behind him. He glanced over his shoulder. Brandon? Did he have rockets in his cleats?

Cody chipped the ball over the head of the Panthers outside right defender with his right foot. Brandon took the ball on the run and continued in on goal, the other three defenders scrambling to cut him off. Cody followed as fast as he could.

"I'm in for the rebound," Cody shouted to Paulo.

Paulo nodded and immediately cut behind him to support Brandon in case he wanted to pull the ball back. Brandon was on a mission, however. He lowered his right shoulder and barged into the box. Cody worried Brandon was so angry that he'd take a needless yellow card. Brandon seemed determined to get a shot off. The goalie came out, and the defender slid with his right foot outstretched in a last-ditch attempt to block the shot.

"Well done, Lions!" a voice called out.

Brandon had back-heeled an inside pass with his left foot to Paulo just before the defender took his feet out from under him.

"Play the advantage," Cody heard Trevor tell them.

Paulo took the ball with his left foot and darted around Brandon and the defender, who were tangled together on the ground. The goalie crouched low, his eyes shifting left and then back to Paulo. Jordan was hovering at the top of the box, so Cody went hard for the front of the net. A second defender lunged at Paulo.

"Cody," Paulo cried.

Paulo snuck the ball with his left foot around the defender to Cody. It was an easy one-timer. Out of the corner of his eye Cody saw Ryan camped out a few metres from the far goalpost. He'd beaten all the other Lions forwards to the spot. Cody curled his left foot and slipped the ball to him.

The goalie's head dropped to his chest. There was nothing he could do but watch in dismay as Ryan redirected the ball into the wide open net.

The Lions parents let out a roar and started clapping. It had been a great goal — maybe the best of the season. The Lions players stared at each other, not sure how to react. The Panthers goalie stomped to the back of his net to dig out the ball.

"Pitiful," a defender muttered.

Cody figured it would look weird not to congratulate Ryan. He walked over. Cody decided a low-key 'nice goal' would do the trick.

"Nice goal," Cody said to Ryan. "I thought I'd passed it too hard."

Ryan shrugged. "It was a gimme. No big deal."

Cody held out a hand down low. Ryan hesitated and

then slapped it halfheartedly. Brandon came over.

"Nice marker, Ry," Brandon said.

He and Ryan slapped hands — for real this time — and they headed back to their end.

"You're welcome," Cody sighed.

Paulo came over. "Nice pass," he said with a crooked smile.

Cody shrugged. "Score's 5–0, and this is more painful than getting a cavity filled at the dentist."

"We're gonna win. That's all that matters," Paulo said.

Their teammates had already gone back to their end.

"You two can join our team if you want," a Panthers defender grinned.

Cody grinned back. "We got the breaks today. The ball's bouncing our way. One of those games."

The defender shrugged. "Don't know about that. You guys are solid. I think it'll come down to you, United, and maybe the Storm. I hope not the Storm, though. Those guys are jerks."

"We agree with that," Paulo said.

"You guys play like a team," the defender said. "That's why you're hard to beat."

"Thanks," Cody said. "I . . . Thanks."

If he only knew the truth! Paulo and he jogged back slowly. Cody looked over at Paulo. They'd met because of their love of soccer. Two kids had stolen Paulo's soccer ball in the park, and Cody had gotten the ball back when they weren't looking. Cody had also asked Trevor to give Paulo a tryout. He really admired Paulo, for his skills and how confident he was with people. He never seemed to doubt himself. He did what he wanted and said what he wanted.

Cody wished he could be like that.

He knew how strongly Paulo felt about the fight to keep UPW from polluting Lake Tawson. He also knew Paulo loved playing for the Lions.

"Have you thought about what William and Brandon and ... the others said about your Facebook post?" Cody asked.

Paulo pressed his lips together. "Sure. Of course."

"And?"

Paulo hesitated. "They should step up and represent," he said. "I don't get why they won't play. How can anyone support UPW?"

He wasn't changing his mind any time soon. "Then what happens to the Lions?" Cody asked.

"Sometimes you gotta stand up for what's right," Paulo said solemnly.

They crossed centre and Paulo took a spot off to the left. Cody kept his eyes to the ground. Standing up to others wasn't exactly what he did best. Cody hated when kids didn't get along, and always had.

Besides, he wasn't sure who was right.

Did he have to choose between Lake Tawson and the Lions?

He couldn't do that.

So what was he supposed to do?

The referee placed the ball on the centre dot and blew his whistle. The Panthers forward passed it to his right, and the other forward fired it to his centre right midfielder.

"Play smart, Lions," Trevor said, his hands cupped around his mouth.

Cody forced himself to pressure the ball. He couldn't wait for the game to end.

Cody dribbled the ball along the water's edge.

"Missed you yesterday," Luca said, shifting over to mark him.

"Yeah — had to do a few things with the family," Cody said.

"Did your Mommy make you a sandwich and tuck you into beddy?" Luca grinned.

The reality was she'd ordered him to stay home to rest. "I . . . I maybe had a couple sandwiches," Cody said, trying to make a joke of it.

Luca laughed. Not the best joke in the world, but at least he didn't dork out like usual. Besides, everyone had missed a few days — except for Mandy, of course. They'd been playing for two weeks now.

A wave washed up on the shore.

"Got ya!" Luca cried.

They'd come up with a bunch of new rules. The water was out of bounds, so big waves made the field narrower. They called that the lake side. On the forest side, they'd collected a pile of branches, logs, and rocks to make a short wall, and you were allowed to bounce the ball off the wall and keep going.

"I'm well rested," Cody said. "Take that."

He back-heeled the ball to Kenneth, who had cut across from the forest side, lifting it slightly so it wouldn't get bumped by the footprints in the sand. Luca shifted over to cover and Kenneth sliced it back to Cody, and he immediately fired it cross field to Mandy camping out by the forest side. She took it nimbly with the inside of her right foot. Cody ran in support a few metres back to give her a passing angle, with Kenneth up the middle, edging slightly to the forest side. Cody grinned: a perfect triangle. The ball went from Kenneth to Cody and back to Mandy.

"Stop pretending you're controlling the ball and make a mistake already," Luca said, all the while watching Cody warily.

"How about we take a break?" Talia said. "Looks like the picnic's a bust. We don't have to keep playing in case more people come."

All morning a few dozen people wearing green T-shirts with lettering that read UPW LOVES WATER had been setting up tents, barbecues, and a big stage with speakers. No one else had turned up. The picnic was supposed to officially start in twenty minutes. Cody figured a quick dunk in the lake was in order.

"What's that?" Kenneth asked.

"It's coming from the parking lot," Mandy said.

Cody heard the drumming, too, and it was getting louder.

A man marched down the sand dune. He was dressed in a bright red jacket with massive gold buttons and matching pants with a black stripe down the sides, and he carried a long silver pole topped with a figurine of two people dancing, which he pumped up and down with each step. Behind him, a band marched in groups of two, and then a whole crowd of people followed them over to the stage.

David kicked his feet dry and walked over from the lake. "So they win best marching band," he said.

"Maybe the picnic's not a complete bust?" Talia said.

"Should we bother playing?" Jordan said. "This is an invasion."

"Let's get the signs and chant 'down with UPW' as they go by," Mandy said.

"There are hundreds of people," Talia said. "Not sure waving two signs will scare them away."

"Something tells me they're marching past us on purpose," Paulo said. "They all could've parked in the main lot."

"If UPW is trying to prove they have way more support than us, they're doing a good job," Kenneth said.

"We have to do something," Mandy said, clearly frustrated. She closed her eyes, fists clenched, and kicked at the sand.

The band set up on the stage and people began to sway to the beat. Soon more and more people streamed onto the beach. Even more people were coming from the main parking lot.

"What's the score?" Cody asked.

"It's 182 for Sad and Pathetic and 175 for the McStompers," Mandy said. She'd appointed herself official scorekeeper.

"Unless the McStompers wanna quit, I say we should keep playing," Cody said. "That's what Percival would want, anyway."

"Charlotte would want all of you to carry me around on your shoulders," Kenneth said. He looked around. "I'm not sensing much support for what Charlotte wants."

Cody kicked the ball to the McStompers' end.

"You take it out," Cody said. "We're winning."

Cody skipped backward to defend. When he turned around a sour taste rose in his throat. Timothy and his crew, along with an older kid he didn't know, were coming over.

Timothy was a stone in his shoe he couldn't shake out.

The boys lined up, shoulder to shoulder, facing each other, Lions against the Storm. Mandy and Talia stood to the side.

Kenneth stepped forward, his arms outstretched. "So delighted you're joining us to fight UPW. Too bad we have a no-loser policy."

"And it's for soccer players only," Luca said.

"So what are you doing here?" Timothy sneered.

"Stopping your dad from destroying the lake," Paulo said.

Timothy froze. "And you're doing that by playing

four-on-four? I keep forgetting how unbelievably lame you guys are. These are the dudes I was telling ya about, Kyle." He nodded to the big kid. Kyle had long surfer-boy hair that hung almost to his shoulders, large cheekbones and big eyes — and thick, powerful legs. He looked like a soccer player.

Kyle looked on without changing his expression. He didn't seem that interested.

"I saw a few guys from the Lions in the parking lot," Timothy said.

"Great. Thanks for that. Bye," Luca said.

"Hey, Jordan. Your BFF, Brandon, is here for the picnic," John said.

"I almost didn't see ya there, Humpty," Timothy said to Cody, "until the shine from your head blinded me. How'd you enjoy your suspension — and the forfeit?"

That got a reaction from Timothy's friends.

"Total punk look."

"Humpty-Dumpty's gonna crack."

"Here come the waterworks, wait for it."

"You're such jerks!" Mandy thundered. "For your information, Cody . . . "

Cody's heart almost stopped. She was going to tell them. Their eyes met — and she laughed. "Cody is ten times the soccer player any of you are."

Silence — followed by a roar of laughter. John needed to hold onto Timothy's shoulder for support. Mandy looked ready to explode.

"Then let's play," Mandy said. She pointed at Timothy. "I saw you against the Lions. You're a total ball hog. You three aren't a big deal either," she said to Antonio, Tyler, and Michael. "And you didn't even play, so I guess you're just useless," she said to John.

The laughter stopped, replaced by cold, hard stares. Timothy kicked at the sand. "I like the sound of that. Four-on-four, call your own fouls, first to score two — and Egg-Head has to play."

"For sure," John said, "and after we'll make egg salad sandwiches outta him."

Timothy gave John a harsh glance.

"Can I pick the rest of the team?" Timothy said.

"Go ahead," Kenneth said.

"I definitely want the ugly stepsisters," he said to Mandy and Talia, with a smirk, "and then I'll go with . . . " He waved a finger in the air. "So many losers to choose from, it's hard. What about you, funny man?" he said to Kenneth.

"He noticed me," Kenneth said breathlessly, clasping his face with his palms.

"Sorry, Jungle Boy," Timothy said to Paulo. "We only play against people who were born here and not in some stupid smelly jungle." He sniffed the air. "Speaking of smelly, John, did you check out the guy's odour?"

"That's so racist, it's . . . " Mandy couldn't finish.

"It's . . . it's . . . it's," John mimicked in a high-pitched voice.

"By the way, I'm getting a wicked whiff of something stinky off Miss Braids. You've heard of showers, right?" Timothy said to Mandy.

"That's why her kind is always doing freaky stuff with their hair. They don't want you to notice the smell,"

Antonio said.

Cody took a step forward and blasted the ball into Antonio's chest so hard he staggered back.

"You're dead, Eggy!" Antonio yelled.

"I wanna see you do it!" Cody yelled back. He stepped forward, enraged, fists ready.

"Hold up, bro," Timothy said. "I'd love to see you waste the guy. We can't fight with our dads and families here. These guys only get tough when we can't fight. Besides, we can settle everything in the game. You lose, you have to stop your stupid Marathon Game until after the vote."

"Mara-lame Game, more like it," John said.

Timothy gave John a pained look. He kicked the ball down the beach. "You can take that end. I assume the water is one sideline and the wall is the other."

"Ball hits the water or hops the wall it's out," Kenneth said.

Timothy shrugged. "So it's me, Kyle, Tyler and . . . Antonio," he said.

Kyle held up his hands. "I know you got a history with these guys and things to settle. It's not my fight, though. I'm gonna get going to the picnic. My folks are there and there are some friends I gotta say hi to."

Timothy stared, wide-eyed. "Kyle, help us out for two minutes. Seriously. We can party all afternoon, no problem. My dad's bringing in some awesome bands and there's tons to eat and stuff. It'll be less than two minutes if you . . . "

"Like I said, not my fight," Kyle said coldly. "Sorry." He took a step away and then turned back. He pointed to Antonio. "Don't really know you, and I know you're Timmy's

130

bud, and I'm his cousin and all, but your comment was totally out of line. You don't talk to a girl like that, at least not in my book. And Tim, you were way off base, too. Like ... doesn't matter where a guy's from. If he can play, he's on my team." He puffed out one cheek, shrugged, and began to walk off.

"Ya ... no problem," Timothy said. "Catch ya later." He waited until Kyle was out of earshot. "Guy's a total flake. Ignore him. Michael, you play."

John's face fell.

Cody could tell Timothy wasn't so confident without Kyle. He must be a really good player. Suddenly, a thought popped into his head.

"What if we win?" Cody said, as Timothy and his team were taking their positions.

"Like that's going to happen," Timothy said.

"Dare to dream," Kenneth said.

Timothy gave the sand a kick, sending up a spray. "We'll clear out to the picnic and you can play your stupid marathon game all you want."

"No. You have to crawl on your hands and knees the entire way," Mandy said.

She sure was tough. Cody always thought girls were kind of sensitive about their looks, more than boys, anyway. Maybe boys only pretended not to care. He sure didn't like people talking about his bald head.

At the other end of the beach, a rock band had taken the stage and people were dancing. Cody caught a whiff of barbecued meat. His stomach rumbled.

Kenneth had the ball. "First to two goals. Last guy back is automatic goalie and can use his hands." He passed to Mandy.

Cody backed up to give her a lane. Here was his chance to make up for his bonehead foul in the Storm game. This was his chance to make up for a lot of things — being afraid of Timothy and his crew and being too scared to stand up for himself.

This was his chance to stop being scared — period.

Kenneth sent Cody a sharp pass, water-side. He brought it down cleanly with his right foot and gave it to Mandy inside. Immediately, she flicked it on to Talia. Michael stepped up. She backed off, and then back-heeled the ball to Kenneth. Cody noticed Mandy slipping up the forest sideline. Cody didn't hesitate. Quick as a flash he powered in between Tyler and Timothy at a forty-five-degree angle. Kenneth placed the ball perfectly. Antonio charged. Cody angled the ball off the outside of his left foot to Mandy veering in off the wing just before running full force into Antonio. They both fell to the sand. Mandy strolled in and scored.

"It's 1–0," she said. "You boys better get your knees sharpened cause you're gonna need them."

Antonio shoved Cody aside and stood up. "No goal. Foul," he said.

"You ran into me," Cody said.

"Players call their own fouls," Timothy said. "Stop your whining."

Cody spit some sand out of his mouth. "Of course you'd cheat. How else could you win?"

"Whatever," Timothy muttered. "Give me the ball," he told Michael.

Michael passed it over. Timothy gave the ball to Tyler

forest-side, who shovelled it sideways to Antonio. He faked an outside move and cut back in. Challenged by Kenneth, he turned and played it to Michael, who made a nice pass to Timothy camped out by the water. Talia was marking him. Tyler pushed forward and Antonio stayed out wide on the forest-side. Timothy's only real play was to put it back to Michael. Cody knew Timothy only passed as a last resort.

Cody swung low to get outside of Timothy's peripheral vision. Talia was a dogged defender, but he figured Timothy would think he could get by her easily because she was a girl. He faked inside. Talia didn't flinch. He did a cross-over and feinted a charge up the shore. She didn't bite. Timothy growled and looked up field — and Cody sprung his trap. He raced over to box him in. Talia saw him coming and pushed forward as well. Their timing was perfect, since a wave had just washed up and Timothy didn't have much room to manoeuvre.

Timothy extended his left arm to keep Talia away. He was so focused on her he didn't notice Cody sneak in from behind. Cody stripped him cleanly of the ball. Tyler was out of the play, and Antonio was too far wide to stop him. Michael backed up, bent low, arms to his sides. Cody stutter-stepped to draw Michael's feet apart and then blasted the ball between them for a goal.

Luca, David, and Jordan let out a huge cheer from the sidelines.

"Special delivery from the mailman," Kenneth said.

"Calm down, losers. I called a foul," Timothy said.

"You're so full of it," Cody spun around and stomped

his feet. "Who cares what you called? Every time you lose the ball you think it's a foul. Here's a news flash. It's not. You're too stupid a player, that's why you lose the ball all the time. You won't pass unless you have to. I knew you couldn't get past Talia, and it was an easy steal — all ball — and a goal. So stuff it — or get yourself a diaper."

Talia smirked, hands on her hips. "You do seem like a big baby," she said to Timothy. "Diapers are probably a good idea. Don't be ashamed. Toilet training takes longer for boys."

"Ha ha," Timothy said.

"Toilet training ain't funny," Kenneth said. "I really think you should try it. Don't you find diapers a pain?"

"And they're expensive," Luca said from the sideline.

"Whatever," Timothy said. "Take the goal. Totally lame, but I don't want Eggy to cry." He brushed past Talia. "Give me the ball," he said to Michael. "Don't be such a sieve. Right through your legs."

"Don't give them a breakaway," Michael snapped back.

Timothy smashed his foot down on the ball. "Let's destroy these losers then get something to eat. C'mon."

Cody covered Tyler. Talia waited for Timothy. Mandy took the forest-side. Kenneth was back as defender–goalie. Timothy glared at them all.

"He's gonna try a bull rush," Cody whispered to Mandy. "I'll slide tackle him then you and Talia should have a clear run on goal."

Mandy nodded ever so slightly.

Timothy dribbled up the field, checking things out, looking right and left. Tyler jogged forward, but Cody let him go, convinced Timothy wouldn't pass. Antonio cut inside and then backed off to the forest-side. Cody didn't move, hoping to draw Timothy closer. The Storm coach sure wasn't teaching triangularity. Tyler was straight in front, which meant Cody blocked any pass, and Antonio was basically level — no angles. Again, all Timothy could really do was put it back to Michael.

Timothy turned to face his own goal, and Cody's heart sank. Of all the times to make the right play! Cody glanced left. Mandy was playing up, still waiting for Timothy to make a charge. He moved even closer to Timothy. It was now or never. Without warning, Timothy spun back and took off with the ball to Cody's left. He wasn't used to playing on a beach with all the footprints, though. The ball popped up and he had to slow down to regain control. Cody slid into the ball, left leg extended. Timothy went flying over him — the ball nestled against Cody's thigh. Mandy took off, as did Talia. Cody jumped up and sent the ball Mandy's way and followed up himself.

Michael came out gingerly, three-against-one. Mandy passed to Talia who raced for the far post. Michael swung across. Talia gave it back to Mandy. A simple one-timer and it would be all over. Michael figured the same and he threw himself across the goal.

"Shoot!" Cody yelled.

Mandy chipped the ball into the middle of the field, five metres from goal, with Michael lying off to the side covered in sand. Cody ran onto it.

"Enjoy," Mandy said.

A jumble of thoughts crowded into his head: how

Timothy had made him feel so small and weak, how much he loved this beach, how much he liked being with his friends, and how important soccer was to him. He stopped the ball on the goal line. Michael scrambled to his feet and dove. Just before his hand got close, Cody back-heeled it in.

"It's 2–0," Cody said. "Have a good crawl."

"You're kidding!" Timothy screamed. "Two fouls in a row!"

"No, we're not kidding," Kenneth said. "You really should try toilet training. Think of the money you'll save on underwear."

Timothy ran at Kenneth, fists ready to throw a punch. Luca bodychecked him to the sand.

"Now that's a foul," Luca said, "in case you were wondering."

Tyler took a step toward Luca.

"What do you want?" Luca said.

"You're such a loser," Tyler snarled.

They glared at each other.

Paulo, David, and Jordan huddled around Kenneth. Timothy got up slowly.

"As usual, you guys are real tough in a pack," Timothy said. "One day I'll take you guys out one at a time. Your heads will ring for a month."

"One day — but not today," Paulo said.

"Forget you, Jungle Boy," Timothy said. He took a sudden leap at Paulo.

Paulo didn't flinch. Timothy waved him off with the back of his hand.

"Losers," Timothy muttered. "Let's get outta here. Stinks

too much here. You want to cheat to win, fine. Whatever." He headed down the beach.

Antonio blew them a kiss. Tyler and Michael followed without so much as a look. John had been standing on the sideline the entire time. Cody had always thought John was like a second Timothy, a big bully who liked making people feel bad. But that's not what John looked like now. He didn't look angry, more like sad, like he wanted to go home, kind of like how John's dad, Mitch, looked when Ian yelled at him.

"You don't have to let yourself be bullied by Timothy," Cody said. John's face went white as a sheet. "Timothy's a jerk — I think you just pretend to be."

John's jaw slackened. He offered a weak grin. "See ya around, Egg-Head. Grow some hair, why don't you?"

Cody felt sorry for him. The dis meant nothing. He understood John now. They actually had a lot in common. John was as desperate to be accepted and have friends as Cody. The difference was John had to hang with a bad group, while he — well, maybe — had real buds. He watched John walk along the water's edge, head down, kicking his heels into the sand.

"You gonna explain yourself?" Kenneth said from behind.

Cody turned around to a group of grinning faces. "Explain what?" he said.

"When did you become a total wild-man unstoppable soccer maniac?" Kenneth said.

"It was an open net," Cody said, his old shyness coming back.

"Imagine what you could do with hair," Kenneth said.

"Kenneth," Mandy hissed.

Luca stared in shock. Paulo didn't know where to look. Cody was laughing so hard tears were streaming out.

Talia began laughing, then Kenneth and the boys joined, and finally Mandy. Cody couldn't stop, and the more he laughed, the more they did. He tried to think of the last time he'd laughed so much. Had to be before he got sick. He used to goof around with his friends at school at the back of the class. Cody had been wondering what happened to that kid, the Cody who could lose it and laugh like crazy about something stupid.

Maybe that kid hadn't gone anywhere?

14

Cody dug the corner of his sweat-soaked shirt into his eyes to wipe away the sunscreen.

"Why's the sun so hot?" Luca said.

"It's like a billion freakin' degrees today," David said.

They'd decided to break early for lunch and were sitting under the tarp.

Kenneth leaned against a cooler, gasping for breath. "Did we get transported to a desert?"

"I called my mom to bring more water," Mandy said. "She'll be here around three."

Luca yawned, raised himself up on one elbow, and then collapsed back to the sand.

"I'm having one of those moments," Kenneth said. "Who's gonna step up and help me?"

Cody was thinking the same thing. *One of those moments*

was their code for *I feel like quitting*. Three long, tiring days had passed since the picnic, and the awesome feeling of beating Timothy and his crew had melted away under the brutal sun. There was one good thing. The anti-UPW protests were growing. The night before almost five hundred people gathered at City Hall Square. Mandy's mom made an emotional speech about keeping water clean for the children. Anti-UPW websites had sprung up all over too. It was hard to tell if UPW, and the mayor and the councillors, were taking any notice, or if they even cared, but it was nice to see. Of course, that didn't help them play in this heat.

Usually, Mandy fired them up when *one of those moments* hit. Kenneth and Talia sometimes did, too. This time no one answered.

"Umm, hello?" Kenneth said. "Help?"

"Too hot," Luca said. "I'm helpless."

"Who's that?" Talia said.

Cody turned and saw four boys coming over. One was carrying a large duffle bag.

"You guys wouldn't happen to have some homemade lemonade with crushed ice, a slice of lime, and a little umbrella?" Kenneth said.

"I'll have one, too," Luca said.

Cody did a double-take. One of the boys was Timothy's cousin. Kyle stepped forward. He ran his hand through his hair.

"Sorry, bro. Shoulda thought of that on a day like this. We just brought some plain H_2O." Luca groaned and Kyle laughed. "Also, sorry for Tim the other day," Kyle continued. "He told me about the game — something about you not calling fouls? That guy thinks there's a foul every time he touches the ball. Been like that since we were kids."

"Is Timothy that cousin of yours — Mister Loud Mouth?" the boy carrying the duffle bag asked. He dropped it to the sand. He was shorter than Kyle, with black hair and wide-set eyes, and he wore grey baggy shorts that fell to below his knees, and a muscle shirt with the logo BOYS UNDER 15.

"I never knew his real last name," Kenneth said.

Kyle chuckled. "He's hard to take. And he's changed lately. He's way harsher, talks racist garbage and gets all aggressive on people for no reason. Gets it from my Uncle Ian. Let's just say we're not proud of all the members of our family. Anyway, let me introduce Hector." He patted the boy on the back who'd carried the duffle bag. "And that's Richard and S.J."

The boys nodded.

"Welcome to the Marathon Game," Talia said. "You don't by any chance play soccer?"

They grinned.

"We play a bit," Kyle said.

"Is that shirt for real or did you buy it?" Kenneth asked Hector.

"Little bit of swag from a tournament we were in," Hector said.

"I claim him for our team," Kenneth said.

"What's the shirt for?" Paulo asked.

"It's the under-fifteen national team," Kenneth said.

Paulo let out a whistle. Now Cody understood why Timothy had wanted Kyle to play so badly.

"Kyle and I are from around here, although we play on different club teams. Richard and S.J. are hanging out for a week or so. We just finished training with the national junior squad," Hector said. "Kyle told us about your game, and we all read your Facebook page and website and thought it was totally cool, and we want to help."

"Your page says the game's open to everyone, so . . . we're here," S.J. laughed.

Cody joined in the cheers. Four guys weren't going to bring UPW to its knees, but it still felt good that someone was listening. Plus it would be totally cool to play with such awesome guys. The junior national team — wow! Hector unzipped the duffle bag and pulled out some baseball caps and a couple of soccer balls.

"We told Coach Blake about the Marathon Game and he donated these balls and hats to the cause; and he made us promise to tell you he's with ya," Hector said.

They cheered again and Hector tossed the hats around.

"So who's in charge?" Kyle said.

They all pointed to Mandy.

"Hardly," Mandy said, red-faced.

"You have two teams, right?" S.J. said to Mandy. "The McStompers and the Sad and Pathetic Football Club?"

"I definitely want to be sad and pathetic," Kyle said. "It's been a lifelong dream of mine."

"Me, too," Hector said.

"What's the score?" S.J. asked.

"It's 276 for Sad and Pathetic versus 268 for the McStompers," Mandy said.

Kyle pointed to the pink shovel sitting on top of a large

mound of sand. "I assume there's a story behind that?"

"That's Pinky, bro," S.J. said. "Didn't you read the blog? Winner gets Pinky — the most prestigious trophy in soccer."

Hector put his hand to his heart. "I never thought I'd get so close."

Cody had to laugh. He'd gotten so used to Pinky perched up on the sand that he didn't notice it anymore. It was totally ridiculous.

"Maybe we should make the field bigger with six-a-side," Paulo said.

Everyone thought that was a good idea, and they got to work moving the wall closer to the forest.

Mandy was tugging on a log. Cody went over to help, but Kyle beat him to it.

"So are you Sad and Pathetic — or a McStomper?" Kyle said.

She laughed. "I'm more the S and P type."

"Awesome. We can be sad and pathetic together," Kyle said. "Who else is on our team?"

"Cody is," she said, nodding at him, "and Jordan and Kenneth."

"So this is the famous Cody," Kyle said. "I hear you and Timmy are good buds."

"Me and Timothy?" Cody exclaimed.

"I think he's joking," Mandy said.

Would he ever stop being so lame?

Kyle laughed it off. "If it makes you feel any better, Uncle Ian came by the house last week and they were talking about playing you guys, and he was all freaked about trying to stop you from scoring, you and that kid over there."

"That's Paulo," Cody said.

"Uncle Ian's racist, and he thinks it's cheating to have a Brazilian on your team — like how is that cheating?" Kyle shook his head in amazement. "But I figured that meant the guy can really play. We did a tour of Brazil last year, and you wouldn't believe the skill level. I saw guys playing on the beach who you'd swear were on the national team." He reached his hand out and Cody extended his, although he had no idea why they were shaking hands.

"I also heard that you and Timmy had a little tussle," Kyle said.

Mandy laughed. Cody wished he could be more like Kyle, able to meet new people without becoming a nervous wreck. Why was he so serious? He didn't feel like that on the inside.

"Not the smartest thing to do," Cody said. "I got a red card, and then we had to forfeit our next game because we only have eleven players on our team."

Kyle and Mandy dragged the log over.

"Timmy needs a good smackdown every once in a while — and maybe more than that," Kyle said.

In five more minutes they'd made the field big enough. Cody spotted a ball and began dribbling toward his end. After playing so much recently, it was weird how differently he felt with the ball on his foot — it was more natural. He found himself reacting instead of thinking. Even skills like bouncing the ball on one foot were way better.

"Yo, feed me."

Kyle side-stepped toward the water. Cody passed it over, but he was so worried about making the perfect pass that he mis-hit it and the ball sailed wide right into the water. Kyle waited for a wave to bring it back. Cody was disgusted with himself. A simple pass and he'd messed it up. Kyle probably thought he was useless.

Kyle came across the beach with the ball, did a spin, flicked the ball up on his right heel and whipped it over his head, and then punched a hard pass to Cody. He reached out tentatively with his left foot. The ball grazed the inside of his boot and went between his legs. Cody wanted to scream he was so embarrassed.

"Nice," Hector said from behind. He tapped the ball between his feet as he went to the Sad and Pathetic end.

Hector thought he'd meant to do that. Cody took a deep breath. He needed to pull himself together. Otherwise, they'd think he was the ultimate doofus and that Timothy was right about him.

Mandy walked by. "Take it easy, Cody," she said. "Just play your game." She was gone before he could respond.

He wasn't sure what game that was. These were junior national level players! And they went on a tour of Brazil? The farthest he'd been for a tournament was three hours on the highway. They seemed like really nice guys, though.

The ball hit the back of his foot and bounced to Paulo.

"My bad," Kyle called out. "Didn't see you weren't ready."

The game had started and he was daydreaming — hardly Kyle's fault. Cody peeled wide left, forest-side, and forced

Paulo to reverse the ball to S.J. He relayed it to Richard, who pushed forward and fed David up the middle. He back-heeled it to Talia cutting behind, and she one-timed the ball to Paulo. He tore down the lake-side.

Cody punched his own thigh and gave chase. Daydreaming again — or too busy watching. It was like he'd forgotten how to play. Mandy came over to slow Paulo's progress and that let Cody get back to take Mandy's spot in the middle. S.J. cut in front of him and Paulo delivered a nice pass for him to run onto. Cody sprinted with everything he had, hoping to stop S.J. from getting a clear shot on goal. He actually arrived first at the ball. Cody fed it back to Kyle, who'd camped out close to the goal.

"Nice hustle," Kyle said to him. He pulled the ball across his body with his left foot and headed toward the forest. Hector fanned out that way and Kyle passed it up. Mandy presented herself inside and Hector gave it to her. Cody had followed the play. Mandy gave him the ball. Cody gave it right back to Mandy, which was the right play because Hector had some space farther up the beach about three metres from the forest wall. Mandy chipped it over David's head. Hector brought it down easily with a raised right foot. Again, Cody followed, and by doing so formed a triangle with Hector and Mandy.

The next moment the ball was on his foot. This was getting kind of fun.

"Yo. Use me," he heard Kyle yell.

Cody launched a left-footed strike wide left to Kyle, and off he went with Paulo hustling to keep him outside. Hector stayed wide right, and Mandy, too. Kyle needed support. Cody put it into high gear and powered down the centre of the field.

"Use me," he called, and Kyle cut the ball inside. Cody sidestepped right and dribbled up the beach-side, *one of those moments* long forgotten in the joy of playing soccer with great players.

The next four days were so filled with soccer that Cody barely remembered them. He was either playing down at Lake Tawson or at a Lions practice. His mom and he were fighting a lot about him being too tired. She had made him come home early yesterday afternoon — and he'd taken the expected razzing. The council vote was going to happen four days from now, so Cody felt guilty when he wasn't at the Marathon Game.

Right now, he was in the middle of some heated soccer action. Kyle headed the ball down to Cody's feet. Cody didn't hesitate, sending it to Kenneth, who one-timed it to Mandy. Paulo broke off his chase to let David pressure the ball. Mandy moved forward. Cody broke away from S.J. to give Mandy options. She picked Kyle, which irritated Cody for a second until he heard S.J. say, "Tell Cody to slow down. He's impossible to cover." That brought a smile out. He put it into overdrive to get clear, and Kyle gave him a nice pass down the lake side.

Cody used to tire after long runs — not so much anymore. Over the past three weeks they'd turned into running machines. Even David, the Lions goalie, was getting better with his ball skills. Plus, playing with the junior national boys had raised everyone's level. It was kind of cool to know they could keep up with players of that quality. Cody had come to realize that it wasn't enough to love the game, and that two practices and a game per week didn't cut it. The hours of soccer at the Marathon Game on top of practices seemed to have done something to him. The game was easier, and the ball felt natural on his feet. At the last practice, Trevor had even complimented the guys from the Marathon Game on their stamina and good decision-making — triangularity didn't seem like such a crazy word anymore. He would've been totally stoked for their next game, if the boys could only forget about UPW and get along. He'd begun to give up on that happening, however.

Cody hesitated, stepped over the ball, and then cut inside, slipping past S.J. David came out, hands low. The next instant Cody's feet slid out from under him and the ball rolled to Luca.

"Foul!" Kenneth cried.

Cody knew Talia had touched the ball first — a great defensive play.

"No foul," Cody said. He accepted Talia's outstretched hand and she pulled him up.

"But she's a horrible monster who tripped you and

probably all sorts of other stuff I didn't see, and she deserves to be punished," Kenneth said.

"Sorry," Cody said. "She got the ball first."

"But we're losing by one goal," Kenneth whispered loudly enough for everyone to hear.

Cody laughed and jogged back to defend. Luca had passed to Richard, and he was bringing it slowly up the forest side.

"Nice pass," Cody said to Mandy.

She scowled. "Should've done it faster. Next time."

That's how the games had gone lately. Fast passing, quick decisions, and hard defending. Goals that used to come in buckets were now hard to come by. No one got tired, and once ball possession was lost it was hard to get it back.

Richard fed Paulo. He threatened to knife in between Cody and Mandy, but Mandy shifted over and forced him back. He passed to Luca, lake-side. Jordan was there to mark him. A wave washed up, taking away his outside move.

A murmuring from the forest caught Cody's attention. Luca put his foot on the ball and looked that way. Jordan looked up, also. Cody wondered what was going on. He didn't see anything, but the murmuring grew louder.

"You hear that?" he asked Paulo.

Paulo turned his head sideways to listen. "Alien invasion?"

"Maybe UPW is having another picnic?" Cody said.

The sound was unmistakable. It was a crowd. The game had stopped and all eyes were on the sand dune. He and Paulo were closest. They wandered over. Cody heard singing. Did UPW hire a choir this time? At first it was too faint to hear the words, and then suddenly he could make it out.

"It's that stupid song Kenneth and Luca came up with!" Cody said. Talia had posted it on their Facebook page for fun. "Why would a UPW choir sing that?"

WE PLAY IN SAND, WE PLAY WITH A BALL,

WE EAT ICE CREAM, AND THEN WE FALL.

UPW IS DUMB AND DINKY,

GO AWAY — YOU STUPID STINKY.

A boy crested the dune. He looked to be about fifteen, athletic, with blond hair and pale skin, and he was carrying a poster that read,

U = UNWANTED

P = PUTRID

W = WATER

A bunch of kids followed, all in shorts and soccer cleats, and all carrying signs with slogans, such as UPW GET OUT, SAVE OUR WATER, and WE LOVE LAKE TAWSON.

"Hey, guys. I'm Philip. Do you know where I can find the Marathon Game?" the blond boy said.

"Not really, but you can play with us," Paulo grinned, and the two boys shook hands.

"This is Ashwin," Philip said. "I'm embarrassed to admit that I know him."

"I'm embarrassed to admit he knows me, too," Ashwin joked.

"Our stupid city council voted for UPW yesterday," Philip said. "But we figure if we can't stop them in our town, maybe we can help you guys."

"We've been following the Marathon Game on Facebook and finally organized ourselves to get over here," Ashwin said. "Our city council totally sold us out. Didn't even tell us the vote was happening. It was over before we knew it happened. Anyway, have you guys really been playing for two weeks?"

"Actually, it's been three," Cody said.

A pile of kids walked by, all carrying coolers and backpacks. They said hi, continued onto the beach, and began talking to the others.

"Hey, Isaac. Come here," Philip called out to a fairhaired, tall boy, thin but strong-looking. Isaac's smile was warm and friendly. Cody took an instant liking to him.

"You guys are our heroes," Isaac said. "Anything we can do to help, tell us."

"Would it help to throw Ashwin in the lake?" Philip asked.

Cody figured Philip and Ashwin were buddies. They kind of joked around like Kenneth and Luca. Cody had always wanted a friend like that — a best friend.

"It's roasting hot on this beach, especially once you start

running around," Paulo said. "You'll be throwing yourselves in pretty soon."

About fifteen kids were milling around, sorting out
their stuff. They'd brought balls and coolers and one girl,
with jet-black hair tied in a tight ponytail, was handing
out FERGUSON AGAINST UPW T-shirts.

Cody did a double-take. He used to live in Ferguson
before he'd moved to be close to the hospital.

Ashwin took a few steps toward the lake. "I actually remember coming here with my family — it's been a bunch
of years, though," he said.

Philip staggered back, as if he'd been punched. "You're
supposed to be my friend, and you dare to sneak past me
so you can jump in the lake before me and be crowned
King of the Lake Jumpers!"

Ashwin and Philip stared at each other. They each let
out a warcry and sprinted toward the lake.

"They're sorta like . . . idiots," Isaac said.

Cody could tell by the way he said it that he was joking.

Isaac said in a serious tone, "Tell me. What's the situation
at City Hall?"

Before Cody could answer a voice called out: "Hey,
Isaac. You forgot your T-shirt."

The girl with the ponytail came over.

"This is Shannon," Isaac said. "You guys are . . . ?"

Normally tongue-tied around strangers, there was
something about Isaac and Shannon that made Cody
relax. They seemed so friendly.

"I'm Cody, and this is Paulo," he said.

"Nice to meet you guys," Shannon said.

"Our town was divided over this," Isaac said. "It got fairly ugly, even fights outside stores. People put up signs all over and held meetings. It was mayhem."

"Hard to say what's going to happen here," Paulo said. "The anti-UPW side is getting its act together. I heard a group gave the mayor a petition with over one thousand names on it. On the other hand, a lot of people want the new community centre."

"Don't sell yourselves short," Isaac said. "The Marathon Game matters. People were talking about it in Ferguson and it brought a lot of attention to the anti-UPW side. Maybe some councillors will notice and it'll give you the votes you need."

"It better," Shannon said. "You're our last hope. UPW wins this vote, and it's done. Lake Tawson gets an ultra-pure water factory."

"So how'd you get the Marathon Game started?" Isaac said. "It's such an awesome idea."

"I fell in love with it the second I heard about it," Shannon said.

"You tell them," Paulo said to Cody. "It was your idea."

Cody felt like a spotlight had suddenly been turned on. He gathered his thoughts.

"We were all standing on the beach wondering what to do," Cody began. "We figured soccer is what we're best at, and that we could play soccer to get attention for our website and Facebook page. Since soccer is the beautiful game, and this is a beautiful place, it made sense."

A shout interrupted him. Philip had Kenneth on his shoulders, and Ashwin had Luca on his, and they were in the water trying to push each other over.

"I've never been here before," Isaac said. "I only moved to Ferguson a couple years ago. Weird how different it looks in person compared to online. It's way more relaxing — and full of energy at the same time. You know what I mean?"

"I totally do." Cody wasn't going to tell them the whole story. "By the way, I used to live in Ferguson," he said.

Isaac and Shannon stared at him. Cody wanted to smack himself in the head. Why couldn't he learn to shut up? They didn't care.

"You're a Fergy?" Shannon said. She turned to Isaac. "The Marathon Game is really ours, then."

Isaac cupped his hands around his mouth. "Hey, Ashwin. The Marathon Game was Cody's idea — and he's a Fergy!"

Ashwin saluted. "Go, Ferguson!" he yelled.

Philip and Kenneth charged him and Luca.

Isaac grinned and gave Cody an elbow. "I think Lake Tawson is calling all Fergies," he said.

"After me," Shannon said.

She sprinted off. Isaac ran after her, and then Paulo.

Cody hesitated, and then he ran, too. It was boiling hot. Why not take a plunge?

Everyone piled in and began splashing about. Cody dove underwater, and he swung his arms and kicked his legs as hard as he could, enjoying the sensation, until his bursting lungs forced him to come to the surface for a breath.

Philip and Kenneth were singing Queen's "We Are the Champions." Ashwin and Luca were lying in the water.

"How dare you challenge us?" Philip said.

"Aren't you forgetting something?" Talia said. She was on Jordan's shoulders.

"Curse your evil stability and balance," Philip sputtered.

"Attack," Kenneth said.

Philip didn't move. Kenneth leaned his head down.

"That was sorta the cue to attack," Kenneth said.

"I would," Philip said. "Only there's a woman and a man with a camera standing on the beach waving to us."

"Maybe she wants to do a documentary on piggy-back fighting?" Kenneth said.

Philip leaned back and Kenneth slid into the water.

"How are you kids doing?" the woman asked.

"We're doing pretty good," Kenneth said.

"Do you know the kids playing soccer to protest the ultra-pure water factory? I thought it was here. They call it the Marathon Game," she said.

"That would be us, then," Kenneth said.

"Are you not playing anymore?" she said.

"Just taking a break to cool off," Luca said.

"Don't let me stop the fun," she said. She wore a sleeveless white shirt, long white pants with a thin brown belt, and a fancy straw hat with a wide brim and a red scarf tied around the top.

"I'm Ester Brinkman of the Brinkman Report, and I'm doing a story on the people opposed to UPW, and I figured what better way to start than to speak to you kids. Who's the organizer?"

"It was his idea," Isaac said, pointing to Cody. "You should start with him."

"That's wonderful. Can you come up for a moment to chat with me?" she said.

Cody bowed his head and headed over. As he stepped out of the water, he heard Isaac say: "We should probably get things set up, no? We did come a long way to play in the Marathon Game."

"Don't think this is over," Philip said to Jordan and Talia.

"Bring it, blondie," Talia taunted.

"Nice to meet you," Ester said to Cody as she made sure the video camera was fixed on him. "What's your name?"

"Cody — Cody Dorsett."

"So, Cody, tell me why you got involved."

He couldn't tell her why this place was so special — that was too personal. But he thought of something else. "UPW loves to tell people why they're good for the community. They never talk about the dangerous chemicals that come from ultra-pure water. You need to check out our website and Facebook page, and you'll see that UPW has done a lot of bad things. They've polluted lakes all over the world, and we don't want to take a chance with this beautiful lake and this amazing forest and park. So if anyone feels the same and wants to help out, they should come here and play soccer with us. Doesn't matter if you play a lot, a little, or can't play at all. There's a schedule of when we're here on the website — but basically it's every day."

"Interesting," Ester said. "Why a marathon soccer game?"

"We're playing the beautiful game to save a beautiful place," he said.

"That's a really nice way to put it," Ester said. "Thank you, Cody."

Luca and Kenneth had crept over slowly.

"Would you like to say a few words?" Ester said.

"We'd be delighted," Kenneth replied.

Cody was happy to let them take the limelight. They were way better than him at this stuff. At the same time, he was glad he'd had a chance to say his piece. Usually, he froze in situations like that, and hopefully he would convince more people to come to the beach or join one of the other protest groups. Cody looked around. He counted twenty-two kids.

Four days to go. Would all this make a difference?

His mom peeled a banana, cut it, and gave him half.

"I'm full," Cody said, pushing her hand away. Even though their game against the Flames wasn't until later in the afternoon, he was way too pumped to eat more. The Flames were good, but this game was definitely winnable; and he was dying to test his new skills and fitness level in a real game.

"You need your potassium," his mom said, holding her hand out. "Good for your muscles." She looked him over. "You sure have tanned up from playing all that beach soccer. No problem with vitamin D, at least. How's the game going, by the way?"

"It's getting kinda crazed, Mom. You wouldn't believe it. We had over twenty kids yesterday. Apparently, more kids have emailed saying they want to come out; and our online petition has over six hundred names. I never thought people would listen, but they are. One kid, his name is Hector, told me his parents changed their minds because of our website and Facebook page, and they wrote their city councillor and told her to vote no. A TV reporter even came — Ester Brinkman. You can even see me being interviewed on YouTube."

A troubled look flitted across his mom's face. "On YouTube? Can you show me?"

He took her phone and found it quickly.

"Your father doesn't need to see this," she said quietly after watching. "I also don't want you doing interviews without my permission. I don't want your face on the Internet unless . . . "

"Lots of kids did it. No big deal."

"It is to me."

"But . . . "

"I'm not debating this. No more interviews without me knowing or you're not playing anymore."

He dropped it. "I gotta go to City Hall," Cody said. "There's a UPW meeting and we're doing a little protest. Kenneth and Luca wrote this totally funny song and . . . "

His dad came into the kitchen, stuffed his phone in his pocket, and promptly gave Cody a sharp look. "You guys ready?"

"I'm ready," his mom said. "Cody, we'll give you a lift."

"Why wouldn't we give him a lift?" his dad said.

"Cody is meeting his friends there and . . . "

"He's coming to the meeting," his dad said. "Joel is freaking out about the negative press coverage on UPW recently, especially the online stuff. UPW's getting pummelled. Joel wants everyone to come out, including families, to support the project."

"Joel freaks out about everything," his mom said. "Cody doesn't need to come with us, and he said his friends are there to . . . "

"He does, and he will," his dad said. "Cody, bring your soccer stuff in case it goes late."

"I can't go to a UPW meeting," Cody gasped. "I've been . . . We've been playing soccer non-stop to show how much we hate UPW and . . . we have an online petition and lots of kids coming to the beach and . . . "

"I don't want to hear it," his dad interrupted. His face was beet red. "Do as you're told. You're part of this family, and I need you to get dressed and support me. I let you go to that beach game, even though Joel threatened to fire anyone caught with a kid playing in it — so this is the least you can do for me."

"Joel has no right to do that," his mom said. She looked furious.

"Joel does what he wants," his dad said.

Cody looked at his mom in desperation.

"Let's get going," his mom said.

He stared at her. He couldn't believe it. "If my friends find out . . . "

"Let's go," his dad said. "We'll be late."

"But, Mom?"

"Run up and brush your teeth," she said, "and then hurry back. We have to go."

She nodded toward the stairs. Cody banged the table with

his fist and stomped out of the kitchen. Halfway up the stairs he heard his mom ask, "Sean, is this really necessary?"

"It's no joke, Cheryl. Joel's on the warpath and looking for an excuse to get rid of people. The UPW contract is not nearly as big as we thought. UPW keeps cutting the price. I know it's unfair to Cody. I feel terrible about asking him to do this. Joel will be watching, though, and I'll . . . I'll make it up to him later."

Cody went into his bedroom and lay down on his bed. His head throbbed. This was impossible, ridiculous. Timothy might be there, and it would get back to his friends and then what could he say? Kenneth and Luca, everyone, they'd lose total respect. Over and over he tried to think of how to get out of this. Fake being sick? They wouldn't let him play against the Flames. Why couldn't his dad just tell Joel to stuff it? Why was he so afraid of that guy?

"Cody!"

He got up and brushed his teeth, grabbed his soccer kit, and went downstairs. His parents stopped talking when they saw him. Not a word was spoken as they drove to City Hall. They walked across the Square and into the main entrance. The doors were huge, and they led to a large dome-shaped hall, with wood panelling on the walls, grey-white marble flooring, and interior windows that stretched from floor to ceiling. Cody looked through the windows into a large, circular room.

"That's the council chamber," his dad said, "where the councillors vote."

On the right, a wide sweeping staircase led to a second floor.

"I think we have to take those stairs," his dad said.

Cody froze in his tracks. A song filled the hall.

UPW GO AWAY,

COME AGAIN ANOTHER DAY,

TAWSON AIN'T NO GARBAGE BIN,

SO WE WON'T QUIT, AND YOU WON'T WIN.

Kenneth, Luca, and Paulo broke away and came over. Mandy and Talia waved. Kyle and Hector held signs.

"We waited for you as long as we could," Kenneth said to Cody.

"We've been at the north entrance. That's where the mayor and councillors go in. We're just wandering around now," Paulo said.

"They won't let us in the meeting," Luca said. "Invitation only."

Cody could barely breathe, and his mind was too numb to talk.

"Hi, Cody's parents," Kenneth said. "How's it going?"

"It's going," his dad said. "Please excuse us. The company I work for is involved, and we have to go to the event." He eyed Cody closely. "All of us are going."

"Cody? You're going?" Paulo said, as if not believing what he'd heard.

"The family was invited," his dad said, "so yes, Cody's going."

"It's just a general sort of thing, nothing too dramatic," his mom said.

"Ya, but . . . didn't you see Cody's interview on You-Tube?" Paulo said. "It's had something like five thousand hits already."

Cody looked up to the ceiling. Thick wood beams spanned the length of the hall, like what you'd see in a ski chalet.

"What interview?" his dad said.

"Check it out," Paulo said. "Cody was awesome. It went totally viral."

His dad grunted.

"Okay . . . Well . . . We'll see you later, Cody," Kenneth said.

Luca was looking at the windows.

"Sure. Okay. See you at the game," Cody said.

Talia and Mandy came by.

"C'mon guys," Mandy said. "Let's go upstairs and sing the song. They'll hear it inside, and I bet there are some reporters."

"We really should go," his dad said.

Mandy froze. "Cody? Where were you?" she said. "Didn't you get my email?"

"I . . . We . . . " His voice faded.

His dad took him by the arm. "Nice to meet you all," he said, pulling Cody firmly to the stairs.

Cody looked back. Mandy's face fell.

"You're not seriously . . . Are you kidding me? After all this, you're switching sides? Seriously?" Mandy yelled.

"Forget it," Talia said.

"No chance," Mandy fumed. "Spineless jellyfish! Don't bother showing up tomorrow — or any day. Thanks for nothing, liar!"

Cody forced himself to walk up the stairs. She was right. He was spineless, only something wouldn't let him stop. He couldn't do it to his dad, not even if it meant losing the respect of his friends.

They were a family.

A large placard directed them into the council chamber. Cody felt like a robot. He couldn't think or feel. He knew he was walking and he could see everything, of course. The room was full of people. The mayor was standing behind a podium, surrounded by a group of people, including Ian and Mitch. Nothing seemed real, though, as if his brain couldn't make sense of it.

"Your friends are over there," his mom whispered. "Do you want to sit with them?"

Brandon, William, Ryan, Jacob, and Austin sat in a row, about halfway up. Austin turned and their eyes met. Austin elbowed William, and they all whirled around to look.

A man approached, tall, overweight, his face puffy, with heavy bags under his eyes.

"Sean, I'm glad to see you're here ... with your family," the man said. He licked his lips and smiled slyly, nodding slowly to his dad.

"Hi, Joel," Sean said. "Not sure if you've met my son, Cody."

Joel's eyes closed briefly. "Not in person, but I've seen your face all over the place, on TV, Facebook, YouTube. I assume you've come to your senses?" Joel crossed his arms and let out a long, loud sigh.

"We encourage Cody to explore his own views," his mom said.

Joel blew air through his lips. "He can explore video games. This isn't a kids' issue. And that stupid soccer game is getting way too much attention, which I still can't believe. The world is so stupid. Bunch of kids play soccer and they're heroes. They should be working. I always had a summer job. All they do is surf the web and watch cat videos . . . and do the Facebook." He scowled. "So that'll be enough of that, right, young man?"

Cody wanted to tell him where to go so badly it hurt. "I'll try," he said. Not exactly a lie since he couldn't go back to the Marathon Game anyway.

Joel seemed satisfied. "Good. That soccer game is a pain and so are those kids."

Cody heard them singing from the hall. Joel's face twisted in anger and he threw his hands in the air. "Where's security? Those kids should be dumped on the sidewalk."

"This is a public building," his mom murmured.

"It's a public building for normal, intelligent, right-thinking people, not idiots," Joel barked. He stomped off.

"You should say hi to your friends," his mom said. William had stood up and was waving him over. "Dad and I will go sit with some people from his work."

Each step was torture. "Hey, guys," he said from the stairs. They spun their knees sideways to give him room to take a seat.

"What's up, bro?" William said. He was half-laughing.

"Not much," Cody said.

William lifted both eyebrows. "I mean, what're you doing here?"

Cody offered a rueful grin. "My dad's company is working with UPW, and he was ordered to bring his family to this meeting — to show support."

"That's the way it is with all of us," William said, "only the other guys don't understand."

"It's like we're the enemy," Ryan said.

"I don't even wanna play our game this afternoon," Austin said.

Brandon leaned over. "They act like we're traitors or something . . . like we're sucks because we aren't at the Marathon Game. My mom's one of the lead engineers and she won't let me. Says it would look bad. I admit at first I was more on UPW's side, or I was thinking that it would be cool to have the community centre and the new fields. I read lots about it, though, including the Marathon Game's Facebook page, and I can see what you guys are talking about. I do. But the Marathon Gamers treat me like I want to poison Lake Tawson myself. Everything's messed up and the team is . . . " He searched for the right word.

"Messed," Cody said.

The place was filling up and the murmuring from the crowd was growing louder. A man at the podium plugged a cord into the microphone. They were going to get started. In the front row, Timothy and John were staring at him. Timothy waved and flashed a thumbs-up.

Cody ignored him. "None of the guys at the Marathon Game think you guys are sucks. That I can tell you. No one ever said anything like that," he said.

"What about Paulo?" William said.

"Some people, like Paulo, are more into the fight and . . . maybe he gets carried away. He doesn't mean it personally. Sounds like he does, but I know him pretty well and he isn't like that. I guess I got carried away, too — and I'm sorry. I'm as guilty as anyone. It's not like you had a choice. Your parents wouldn't let you play. And besides, you should be able to make up your own minds."

"There's that, too," Brandon said.

"It's a disaster," William said. "Worst thing is we gotta listen to all these speeches and they're always so boring. These UPW events are killing me."

"Shush."

An adult gave them a dirty look.

"My dad even admitted to me that he wasn't going to lose his job if the council votes no," William whispered. "It's basically a scare tactic, from Ian and the mayor. They want people to think the world will end if UPW doesn't get a yes, like there's a worldwide shortage of silicon chips."

A woman rose to her feet. "Mayor, I'm Ester Brinkman, of the Brinkman Report. A great deal has been written about the possible environmental impact on Lake Tawson and the surrounding parklands. How can we be sure the UPW water facility will be safe?"

The mayor's smile was enormous. "I'm happy to answer any questions, but perhaps we can leave them to the end."

"It's just one question," Ester persisted, "and you haven't commented on the environmental risks posed by the project, and I think everyone in this room would like to hear your views on the matter."

"Absolutely," the mayor said. "As soon as we've finished the presentation, I'll be happy to speak to you."

Ian came over. "There will be a press conference tomorrow and you can ask your questions then."

"I prefer to ask them now," she said.

Ian frowned. "This is an invitation-only event . . ."

"I was invited," she said, holding a card up.

"Did you actually send her an invitation?" Ian said to Mitch.

Mitch turned beet red. He opened a binder and looked down. "I . . . um . . . we received a lot of requests for tickets and you wanted press coverage and . . . a lot of invitations went out. Hard to keep track of every one of them." He swallowed hard.

Ian rolled his eyes and shook his head a few times.

"So, Mayor, can you answer the question?" Ester said.

The mayor was no longer smiling. "UPW has assured me, and everyone on the project is on side with this, believe me, that they, I mean UPW, will do everything they can to make this project one hundred per cent successful. I can assure you the environment is very important to me, to UPW. Very important. Critical. Lots of planning is going into everything — everything — down to the last nut and bolt. Lots of planning. So believe me when I say there's nothing to worry about. UPW is a first-class company, first class, and so . . . " He looked at Ian.

"We should probably move on. We have a full agenda," Ian said.

"He's not answering," William muttered.

"Can we turn down the lights and start the slideshow?"

the mayor said into the mic. "We have some awesome numbers to show you. Just awesome. We also have some drawings and pictures, which I know you'll love to see. Then we'll hear from Carl Bornsteen, vice-president of international operations at UPW, and he'll bring us up to date on the project. Thanks for your support on this. It's important to get the word out. The vote's in three days and we need you to speak to your councillors and get them on side."

Ester remained on her feet. "Thanks for answering my question, Mayor Winthrop. I really appreciate it."

The mayor nodded at her.

Ian walked over to Mitch and began talking in his ear. Mitch tucked his binder under his arm and lowered his head.

"What's gonna happen this afternoon against the Flames?" William said to Cody.

All the boys leaned in.

"I guess it's gonna be awkward. Only, we gotta ignore all this and win," Cody said.

"It's gonna be a nightmare," Brandon said, "worse than when Ian ran the team."

He was obviously upset, and even though William was better at staying calm, Cody knew he was, too. These guys were loyal teammates, Lions to the core. They'd sacrificed as much as anyone to keep playing with only eleven players. He couldn't blame them for thinking the Marathon Game threatened the Lions' season. Cody knew that sometimes at practice he'd been tired and had let up. Sure his fitness level was way better, and so were his skills. They were playing too much, though, and sometimes it showed on the field. The last couple of weeks couldn't have been much fun for them. Cody was about to find that out first hand this afternoon

The lights dimmed, and a picture of a building appeared through mist floating on the water, with soft music in the background.

"Line it up," Trevor bellowed from the sideline.

David was about to kick the ball downfield. Only a great right-hand save had stopped a sure goal — and only a miracle caused the Flames striker to miss the rebound wide right.

Brandon rushed over to Cody.

"Paulo's dad told me there's only about ten minutes left in the game, plus injury time, which might be another minute or so," Brandon said. "A tie's not good enough, either. It'll kill our playoff chances. We need the win, so it's two goals or we're toast."

Ryan trotted over. "We've had maybe five shots on goal all game," he said. "Can't believe we're losing to the Flames. We should beat them easy."

"That's because we're not passing to each other, at least

not unless we have to," Cody said. His desperation level was about to go off the charts.

"Tell the Marathon Gamers," Ryan said. "I've been open."

"Now do you get it?" Brandon said. "They think we suck because we haven't been playing beach soccer."

"I don't think that's true," Cody said.

The boys took their positions. David sent a line drive to the right side.

"Yours, Paulo," Cody said.

Paulo had barely looked his way all game. It was like they were total strangers.

Paulo broke for the ball and then skidded to a stop. The ball landed between them and bounced to a Flames midfielder. Cody groaned.

"I thought . . . " Paulo turned back to the middle of the field without finishing his sentence.

Cody looked to the sideline. Trevor smacked his clipboard on his thigh. Leandro shook his head and slowly lowered his chin to his chest. Even the parents looked dejected, especially his mom. Usually she was yelling her head off.

The midfielder sent the ball to his inside left defender. Paulo trotted forward slowly. Jordan hung wide left. Cody looked about. His teammates were standing around, with no energy, as if they were waiting for the whistle to blow so they could go home. This wasn't Lions soccer. Maybe they didn't like each other. Maybe they hated each other.

Soccer had to be bigger than that, bigger than teammates having fun together and being friends. It wasn't the beautiful game because you showed up and ran around the field after a ball. It was the beautiful game because eleven guys worked as a unit to win the game. The Lions were disrespecting soccer. They could disrespect each other all they wanted — but not soccer. That was plain wrong.

He'd had enough.

Cody tore past Paulo, forcing the defender to send the ball wide right. Strikers weren't supposed to waste energy chasing the ball — so what? He'd wasted enough time watching the Lions play lousy soccer. Cody continued on. The ball swung wide left and Cody kept going. He was beyond thinking about playing his position. He was going to show the Lions how to respect the game — even if it meant running himself to death. The defender trapped the ball with his left foot. Cody closed in. Ryan sealed off the sideline. Cody cut back, taking away the defender's option to pass back to the goalie. The defender transferred the ball to his right foot.

The Flames defender had to go inside to his left mid-fielder — a lateral pass. Cody leapt sideways and extended his right foot. The defender tried the inside pass anyway. Cody's toe grazed the ball and knocked it sideways. He had the momentum and in two quick steps he'd gained possession.

That would teach the Flames to disregard triangularity!

Cody snapped the ball to Paulo.

"Play soccer, Lions!" Cody barked.

They weren't friends, but they had to start playing for real or he'd totally lose it on them.

"Paulo, inside," Kenneth called.

Paulo gave it up to Kenneth. Pressure surrounded him immediately.

Cody angled over. "I'm here," he said. His lungs were beginning to ache and his thighs were burning.

Kenneth sent it over. Cody turned his left foot inward and one-timed it to Paulo, who'd worked hard to gain some separation from the Flames midfielders. Fists clenched, Cody pushed himself harder.

"On your left," Kenneth called. Paulo delivered another perfect pass and Kenneth set off without having to break stride.

The four defenders were seven metres from the box. Cody launched a full out charge. Kenneth slid the ball to Paulo, and he one-timed a right-footed chip over the top of the back line.

Cody got to it first. The goalie shifted across to face him. Cody could see Jordan at the top of the box, but a defender had turned to mark him. That decided it. He took one step and launched a massive strike with his right foot. The ball hooked left, past the desperate reach of the goalie's right hand. It nicked the bottom of the crossbar — and went in.

"Go, Lions!"

"One more goal!"

"Set up fast. We need the win!"

Cody ignored the Lions parents calling out to them and he continued running to the flag at the far corner. Probably everyone thought he was acting like those guys who go mental after they score. The truth was he needed to be alone, even for a few seconds. This game was so wrong, this team was so wrong — and he felt responsible, not totally, but he'd done his share of the damage. What had he done to make guys such as William and Brandon feel okay about supporting their parents and families? Nothing. What had he done to keep the team together? Nothing.

He'd been content to play in the Marathon Game — so he could feel like he had friends. He was just happy to be included. Selfish, that's what he'd been, too busy blaming Paulo for his Facebook post, or Brandon for losing his temper, or Kenneth for not being a team leader.

He turned around. Kenneth, Paulo, and Jordan were huddled about five metres inside the box. Cody looked over at them. Their eyes met. They'd never understand what he'd gone though. How could they? Only someone who'd had cancer, or someone like Mandy who'd lost her own brother, would get it. Why be afraid of anything after that?

So why be afraid to say what needed to be said?

Eyes ablaze, Cody charged over to them. "We're supposed to be a team!" he barked.

The boys didn't move a muscle.

"We didn't have the right to dis guys because they're helping their families. It's easy to do things when nothing is on the line. Easy to play soccer on a beach when your parents let you, and they pack you a lunch and drop you off and pick you up. Easy when you don't have to worry about your mom or dad losing their jobs," Cody said.

Paulo's eyes softened. "I get that . . . "

"You don't get anything!" Cody snapped. "Your dad's a doctor, so you have no worries. I'm against UPW as much as anyone, but my dad needed me to help him this morning and I did — and I'll do it again. I haven't changed my mind, but I'm not turning my back on my family ever, not for anything or anyone. Do you get that?"

Cody looked down the field and waved. "Lions! Get over here. You, too, David!" he yelled.

They jogged over. He waited until they'd all joined him.

"Soccer is bigger than an argument about ultra-clean water," Cody said. "Brandon, you think the Marathon Game is stupid. Well, it's not. We started the Marathon Game to save a beautiful place with the beautiful game, and not because we think you or anyone else on the team sucks." He turned to Paulo, Kenneth, and Luca. "Can you tell me what's so beautiful about this game or what's so beautiful about the way we've been yelling at each other the past three weeks? And what's so awesome about a beach soccer game? Why does that make you special? The Marathon Gamers have been acting like Timothy and Antonio and the rest of them — with no respect for the game — no respect for the team."

Cody's body shook he was so angry. How'd it all go so wrong, so fast?

"We don't have to be friends. Fine. But we have to be Lions. We have to play soccer the way it's supposed to be played. I remember how we won that tournament — together — as a unit. If this is how we're going to play from now on, I'm outta here. Seriously. Just tell me, and I'll get off the pitch right now, and you won't see my bald head again. This ain't worth it. I'll find a real team — or I'll quit playing."

"No one wants you to quit . . . "

"I disrespected guys on this team," Cody continued, cutting off Kenneth. "I was too full of myself about being a Marathon Gamer, and I'm sorry for that. My bad — totally. I'm not speaking for anyone else. I don't have the right. This is just me. But I wanted everyone to hear me say that." He took a deep breath. "The way I see it, we either play together or let the Lions die already."

The referee blew his whistle.

"Line it up, Lions," he called out. "Enough celebrating."

Paulo had been looking down at the ground the whole time. He lifted his head. His face was deeply flushed. "I've been the worst one. I've been a bad teammate. And . . . there's no excuse for that. Guys, I'm sorry. I was . . . I acted like a jerk. I get like that. Don't know why. I get so stubborn, and even when I know I'm wrong, I won't admit it. Feel free to tell me to shut up from now on."

"First off, shut up, Paulo," Kenneth said. The guys laughed a little. "Second, I was an even bigger jerk than Paulo. Sorry guys."

Luca slapped his head. "That's just great. I was an even bigger jerk than you, so that makes me the biggest jerk here."

"I wasn't perfect either," Brandon said. "I didn't even try to make things better. I sorta have the same problem as Paulo."

"I said that stupid thing at practice," Paulo said to Brandon. "I didn't mean it. I was just mad."

"Forget it," Brandon said.

He and Paulo slapped hands.

Kenneth held out his hand toward Cody, palm down.

Cody gave him a puzzled look.

Luca reached out and put his hand on top of Kenneth's. Brandon put his hand on next, and then David. Jordan put his arm around Brandon's shoulder and added his hand to the pile. Soon there were ten hands — together. Cody put his on top.

"Give me a roar on three!" Cody yelled.

"One. Two. Three!"

The boys unleashed a massive roar, the loudest ever.

"I said enough celebrating," the referee said. "You're not Manchester United."

"Don't wanna be," Kenneth said. "We're the Lions."

"We are now," David said.

"Once a Lion, always a Lion," Luca said.

"Let's do this thing!" William yelled. "Game's tied 1–1. We gotta win this."

The boys jogged back to their end in a pack.

Paulo elbowed Cody in the ribs. "Nice shot," he said. "You should've angled it more so it hit the crossbar and then the post — more spectacular."

Cody grinned. "I would've if the pass had been better."

"We ready for one more?" Kenneth cried from midfield.

Cody didn't answer. No need. He took his spot on the edge of the circle, flexing his fingers and itching for the kickoff. He guessed they had about eight minutes. He didn't feel the slightest bit tired, just the opposite — full of energy — full of fight.

He felt like — a Lion!

Cody hesitated at the top of the stairs before forcing himself to take the first step. He was tired. He trudged over to
the kitchen.

"I was just thinking about that game yesterday," his
mom said, as he took a seat at the kitchen table.

"We had to win or we wouldn't even have had a chance
to make the playoffs," he said.

His dad came in. "Explain 'injury time' again. Your
mother was babbling about you scoring a last-minute
goal?"

Cody had connected off a wicked corner from Jordan
to beat the Flames. "A game is ninety minutes, but the
time is always running. The referee adds up to four minutes at the end of the game for when the action stopped
because someone was hurt."

"So the game was actually over when you scored?" his dad said.

"Kinda," Cody said.

He and his mom shared a look. They liked to joke about his dad knowing nothing about soccer.

"I was worried your friends were going to crush you after you scored," his mom said. "Do they have to pile on like that?"

"It was a big win," Cody said.

The celebration made it seem like old times, with everyone in a big huddle, jumping up and down, high-fiving, and slapping hands, and parents cheering.

"I heard you yelling at your teammates to come down to the far end after you scored the first goal," she said. "What was that all about?"

Cody wanted to tell her. That was private stuff, though — Lions stuff. "Just a pep talk. We knew we had to win, so . . ."

"What's up this morning?" his dad asked him.

Cody shrugged. "Nothing. Why? Are we going somewhere?"

His dad took a sip of coffee and put his mug on the table.

"You and I are. How about we take a drive?" he said.

"Where?"

"That's what I want to talk to you about," his dad said.

"Another UPW event?" Cody said.

"It's connected to UPW," his dad said, "but I'm not asking you to support them, if that's what you're worried about."

Cody could tell it wasn't the time to argue. He would've preferred to waste the morning gaming. It was hard to believe he and the guys had been complaining to each other the day before the Flames game that the Marathon Game was taking up all their spare time. Not anymore — at least for him. He might've patched things up with the Marathon Gamers on the Lions — but not Mandy. She'd never forgive him. He remembered Mandy's eyes when she saw him walking to the council room for the UPW event.

He'd never forget that.

His dad got up from the table. "Let's go, Cody." He walked out of the kitchen.

Cody looked at his mom and raised his eyebrows.

"See you later, dear." She pointed to the front door. "Your dad is waiting."

She obviously wasn't going to tell him what was going on. Cody followed his dad to the car.

"Why's my bike in the back?" Cody asked.

His dad backed out the driveway and set off down the street without answering.

"Are we going somewhere specific?" Cody said.

"We are."

"And . . . that is?"

"You'll see when we get there, Cody."

That was that. His dad wasn't talking. Cody turned on the radio and flipped around a few stations. Every song sucked. He switched it off. His dad turned right and headed down a hill. Three minutes later he turned toward the lake. Suddenly, Cody got it. His dad was going to try to change his mind about UPW now that the Marathon

Game was done for him — and then make him bike home if he said no. The bike ride didn't scare him. He'd done it tons of times. He looked at the clock in the car: 9:30. Hopefully, they'd called for a later start than usual.

His dad parked near the gate.

"Let's talk a walk to the beach," he said.

Cody was totally confused. This made no sense. His dad didn't seem angry, more like serious. His face was stern, his lips pressed tightly together. His dad reached behind him to the backseat and pulled out Cody's backpack, and then he got out of the car. Cody did too, and followed his dad down the path, steeling himself up for a major lecture. His dad didn't say anything until they'd crested the sand dune.

"You sure do have quite a set up," his dad said.

"We had twenty-two kids the other day," Cody said. "Kinda cool to think how much it's grown. I know you think it's stupid, the Marathon Game, I mean."

"I don't think it's stupid, the opposite in fact," his dad said. "I think it's an incredible thing you kids have done. Amazing. And all by yourselves. You're standing up for what you believe in. What father wouldn't be proud of his son for doing that?"

They continued on to the water.

"I've been unfair to you," his dad said. "You have every right to protest against UPW. I've been so worried about my work, I ignored my most important job, which is being your father."

They stopped a couple of metres from the water. His dad smoothed the sand with his foot.

"Do you remember, about a month ago, after one of

your games, and we talked about you getting sick, and how I didn't handle it well? I turned into a workaholic, at the office all the time, not making enough time for you or your mom."

"Of course I remember, and . . . it wasn't all like that, Dad. You were always there for the treatments and . . . think how many times you brought me here."

"I appreciate you saying that. But I remember what you said when we talked: it was easier for you because you only had to think about getting better, while your mom and I had to worry about you. I've been thinking about that a lot, and it's made me realize that I've become a worrier, afraid of life, afraid for your health, afraid of the future. My worrying has affected the family, in a negative way, just like my working all the time when you were sick affected us, and that's not right." He shook his head angrily and kicked at the sand.

"Is that why we're here?" Cody asked.

"We're here because this is where you belong," his dad said. "I'm not going to be that worrier anymore. I don't want you to be that kind of kid, either, the kid so scared of things he ends up doing nothing. Not my son — he should be the type of boy who stands up for himself and for what he believes in, like what you're doing now." He put a hand on Cody's shoulder. "I'm proud of you, and I apologize for putting you in such a tough spot yesterday. I had no right." He looked at his watch. "I checked the Facebook page this morning. They're coming in about forty-five minutes. I haven't messed things up with your friends too bad, have I?"

"It's a little complicated, Dad, especially with a few people — mostly one, really," Cody said. "I should probably come home with you."

"Would it help if I told that person I made you go to the UPW event?"

"I don't think that's the point, Dad. We're a family and you needed me to go. She may not see it like that, but I do."

"This person is a friend of yours?"

"Not sure. A little. We just met. It's that girl — Mandy."

His dad handed him his backpack. "Try giving her a chance. She may surprise you."

She had before. And everyone deserved a chance.

"I'll talk to her," Cody said.

"Good. I'll lock your bike to the rack in the parking lot," his dad said.

His dad smiled, and they both became quiet. Then they hugged — and Cody held on, he just needed to — because he felt, for the first time in a long time, that his dad was back in his life.

"Your mom packed you lunch," his dad said. "It's in your backpack."

"I'll probably be home soon," Cody said.

"No problem." His dad nodded to the forest. "I should go."

He waved and set off toward the sand dune.

"Dad!"

He turned back.

"Thanks."

His dad smiled gratefully. "You're welcome. See you later."

Cody watched him until he disappeared over the dune. It struck him that he'd never been here alone, not in all this time. A few people were swimming or sitting around, but they were far off, so it felt like the beach was his. He listened to the sounds: the waves, the people, and the wind. His thoughts grew quiet, as if his mind had emptied, and that made it easier to understand what he was really feeling.

People always said he was like his mom, that he looked like her, that he was athletic like her. He had a lot in common with his dad, too. His dad always worried about things: money, his job, and even unimportant stuff like being late for a movie or the car breaking down or whether it would rain. Cody worried a lot also, although funnily enough he never really worried that much about the cancer when he was sick, only after when he felt better. When he was sick he just tried to get healthy. Now that he was healthy, he worried about everything.

He rubbed the back of his right leg and laughed. He used to check his leg about a hundred times a day. He didn't anymore. Must be a good sign. He felt the top of his head. More than peach fuzz, for sure. In another month, he'd have real hair — short, but still real. He sat down by the water's edge and opened his backpack.

They'd be here soon, and he had to think of what to say to Mandy — then he caught himself.

He wouldn't worry about that. He'd tell the truth. He'd tell her how he felt about supporting his dad, and she could accept it or not. If his dad wasn't going to worry about things anymore, neither was he. Cody looked in his backpack. His mom had packed a sandwich, an apple, and some water, along with his cleats and shirt. He'd eat later. Now he was tired. Cody lay back and closed his eyes.

"Yo, bro. Sorry we're late. We met up at the park and cruised down in a pack. Talia got some reporters to film us."

Cody woke up with a start. Kenneth tossed his backpack to the ground. The other Marathon Gamers were close behind.

"My dad dropped me off early," Cody said, rubbing his eyes. He wanted them to hear that his dad had driven him over. Mandy was standing at the back, barely able to look at him.

"Close call yesterday," Luca said. "We nearly blew it."

"Most of us played like garbage," Paulo said, "especially me."

"The Storm will kill us if we play like that, for sure," Cody said.

"A win's a win," Kenneth said. "We need to come out stronger next game. Who's it against?"

"We play United," Luca said. "Huge game."

Talia held out her hands. "Are you guys seriously going to act like nothing happened?" she said.

Kenneth tilted his head back. "That's the basic idea."

"This is unacceptable boy behaviour, even for you guys," Talia said.

"Do we really have to talk about it?" Kenneth said.

"I think I do," Cody said. "I came to say something — and then I think I'll just go. I'm sorry I disappointed you, Mandy. I can't say sorry for going to the council chamber, though. My dad asked me to go, and I needed to help him by being there so he would keep his job." He let himself smile. "I'm just glad you didn't kill me."

"I would've, but you got to the stairs first," Mandy said. She stepped forward. Her eyes were puffy and red. "I acted like an idiot at City Hall and said those terrible things. I didn't mean it. Typical of me, yelling at people and trying make them do what I want. Please don't go."

Cody came over and gave her a hug, and then he hugged Talia.

"Do we all have to hug, or can we go back to my idea and pretend nothing happened?" Kenneth asked.

"I gotta admit I really like Kenneth's idea," Luca said.

"I don't even know what you guys are talking about," Paulo said. He dropped a ball to his feet, and flipped it back and forth a few times. "Can we get marathoning already?"

"Go Sad and Pathetic!" Kenneth exclaimed.

"McStompers rule!" Luca replied.

"I think I'm giving in a bit to your immaturity, but *Pink-y, Pink-y, Pink-y,*" Talia chanted.

They headed to the forest to throw their stuff under the tarp. A hand reached out to pull Cody back.

"I really am sorry," Mandy said. "I don't know what gets into me sometimes. I'm like a monster ready to explode."

"You're no monster," Cody said. "But I think I get how you feel. I got bullied on the Lions a lot, because of my hair, by Timothy and John and their friends. I didn't really get it then — amazing to think it was only a month ago. I used to think I was angry about it, and about getting sick, only now I think I was more afraid than angry. I was afraid of Timothy and his crew, afraid of Ian and Mitch, afraid kids on the Lions wouldn't like me, afraid to make new friends, and I was terrified of the cancer."

"I guess you're right. Maybe it's more about being afraid than angry." Mandy's head lowered. "I'm glad you came back, Cody. I wasn't looking forward to playing today — until I saw you."

"People like you and me, who've gone through it, with sickness and stuff, I think it's easy for us to be afraid of things, and I think that's what makes us sad sometimes. For me, as soon as I'm afraid, I get sad. Then I get scared about being sad. Then I get angry to make it stop. Getting angry doesn't work, though. I think the only way to stop being sad is to stop being scared in the first place." He shrugged and smiled wistfully. "Not sure that makes any sense. I guess what I'm trying to say is I still get scared — but maybe not as often — and that means things are getting better."

Mandy looked up at him. Her deep brown eyes glistened, and her face radiated kindness and, possibly for the first time since they'd met, happiness. "You would've liked Gavin," she said. "You sorta have the same personalities."

"He was super cool, funny, and smart?" Cody said.

She pursed her lips. "Something like that," she said. "I like your idea, though. We'll try not to be afraid, you and me, and maybe, one day, we won't be."

"You guys playing?" Luca called out.

"Go Sad and Pathetic!" Cody yelled.

He held his hand down low, and Mandy gave it a slap.

"Got texts from Jordan and David," Kenneth said as Cody and Mandy walked over. "They're coming later.

Kyle and the boys have training and can't make it."

"The Fergies are coming tomorrow, for the last game before the vote, and also a group from Bowmont," Paulo said. "It'll be fun to play for a few hours with the Original Six."

"What's the score, anyway?" Cody said.

"Does it really matter?" Mandy said.

They all turned, mouths gaping in disbelief.

"Is the world coming to an end?" Kenneth said. He turned to Luca. "Did you notice any zombies roaming around and eating people?"

"I thought I saw one, but it turned out to be you," Luca said.

"For that, I'm totally munching on your arm when I'm a zombie," Kenneth said.

"Don't be such a jerk," Luca said. "I don't wanna be that lame zombie that runs off-balance because he only has one arm. I'll never catch people to eat."

"Sorry. Your arm looks so delicious I won't be able to help myself," Kenneth said.

"It's 343–340 for the McStompers," Mandy said.

"Phew," Kenneth said, breathing heavily, hand to his chest. "Mandy's back. No apocalypse."

"Maybe I'm a little competitive?" Mandy said.

Talia snorted. "And maybe the sun is a little hot?" she said.

"And maybe there's a little water in the Pacific Ocean?" Paulo said.

"And maybe I like to eat cupcakes?" Luca added. He paused. "I killed it, didn't I?"

190

Kenneth nodded.

"I hate myself," Luca said. "Eat this arm and get it over with," he said to Kenneth.

"That's the thing about zombies," Kenneth said, pushing Luca's arm away. "If it's too easy, they won't eat you."

"I'll never get the hang of being a zombie," Luca said.

"You will," Kenneth said. "Zombies are like regular people, except they're dead, they eat people, and they moan a lot."

Paulo kicked the ball toward the far goal. "Sad and Pathetic can kick off since they're losing."

Luca began to sing:

MCSTOMPERS IS MY KIND OF TEAM,

SO PASS THE BERRIES AND WHIPPED CREAM.

Luca's shoulders slumped. "I killed it again, didn't I?"

"You always kill it. But don't worry. You can't help ruining things. It's your personality," Kenneth said.

"You always know how to cheer me up," Luca said. "Thanks."

Mandy nodded to Cody and he smiled back. Happy sure beat sad — hands down. You just had to work at it.

Cody jogged to his end, raising his knees to his chest to loosen up.

19

Cody tracked the loose ball down and sent it wide left to Luca overlapping down the wing. That sent the Rangers defenders scrambling to get back. It had been like this the entire first half: relentless, fast, quick passes, triangularity, and teamwork. Cody couldn't remember if he'd ever had so much fun playing soccer. It really was a beautiful game. And they'd been rewarded with three goals: Kenneth on a massive strike from one metre inside the box, Cody on a header off Jordan's cross, and Paulo on a penalty shot. The Rangers were one of the best defensive teams in the league, which made the three goals even more impressive.

When Cody wasn't near the ball, or there was a stoppage in play, his mind wandered a bit and his nerves kicked in big time. The councillors were meeting at City Hall this morning to vote. It could even be happening now. Every once in a while his eyes would meet Kenneth's or Paulo's or Luca's, and he could see they were thinking the same thing. The hardest part was the waiting — and knowing there was nothing he could do about it.

Luca charged down the field, faked an inside dribble and turned on the jets to the outside.

TWEEEET!

Luca spun around and threw his hands up in the air — and then he laughed. The referee was heading off the field. It was halftime. Cody grinned and held out a hand, and Luca bent down and slapped it.

"I was doing my best Cody imitation and was gonna totally speed burn that stiff and score a spectacular goal," Luca said.

"You've got too much hair for that," Cody joked.

Luca screwed his eyes tightly. "I can see three or four hairs trying to grow. Don't sell your hairdo short."

"Short is the problem," Cody said.

Luca laughed and they slapped hands again. Kenneth and Paulo joined them as they walked off.

"We can't let up," Paulo said. "Next goal puts this away."

"Good hustle up the left side with Luca," Kenneth called out to Brandon.

He and Jordan were walking to the sideline together.

"It's easy when you guys are running their defence to death. I have five wide-open guys to pass to every time I have the ball," Brandon said.

"Hey, look who's playing here next," Kenneth said.

Behind the Rangers net, the Storm had formed a big circle and they were passing the ball around to each other.

"We should invite them for crumpets and tea this afternoon," Luca said.

"Oh, let's do that. We shall. That would be so delightful," Kenneth said, clapping the tips of his fingers together.

"Who are they playing?" Cody asked.

"The Ravens. I can see some yellow jerseys in the parking lot," Luca said.

"Tough game. Ravens are in third, I think," Kenneth said.

"I might have to watch," Luca said.

"I might have to watch you watching," Kenneth said.

"Huh?" Luca said.

"Forget it," Kenneth said. "I have no idea what I say eighty-three per cent of the time — and the other half I'm really confused."

Cody said what he knew was on their minds. "Do you think the vote is done?"

"I ain't gonna think about it," Kenneth said. "I wanna live in ignorance a bit more. We got a game to play."

Trevor and Leandro were waiting for them with water bottles.

"Hustle it up," Trevor cried. He clapped a few times. "Don't say you're tired just because you played an awesome first half."

All the boys hightailed it in.

"Great spacing, boys," Leandro said. He held the whiteboard up. "I just want to go over a couple of ways we can mix up the attack and keep them confused."

Cody leaned forward so he wouldn't miss anything.

"We missed a few fast-break opportunities because we

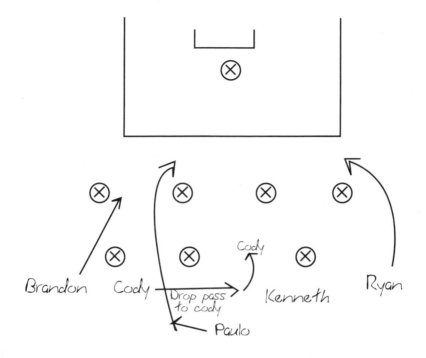

Brandon   Cody

Cody

Drop pass to cody

Kenneth

Ryan

Paulo

let them force us to pass too quickly or to slow it down," Leandro began. "The Rangers like to pursue the ball. This is a misdirection play. It takes advantage of their aggressiveness." He sketched a play quickly. "Assume Paulo has the ball, with Cody in support inside and Brandon and Ryan in support on the outside. Paulo cuts across the field toward an inside midfielder. When he gets close, back-heel a pass to Cody cutting the other way. Paulo continues on into the gap between the outside and inside midfielder. Midfielder closest to the ball overlaps outside, let's say Ryan in this case, and Brandon drives for the inside gap in the backline. Cody can shoot, or pass to

Brandon, Paulo, or Ryan. Make sense?"

It made total sense. Cody could hardly wait to get back out there.

"We don't want to overload you with plays," Trevor said. "You're playing great — and most of all . . . " He paused and looked around.

"Most of all we're playing like Lions!" Kenneth roared.

The boys huddled up, put their hands in the middle, and let out a big roar on three.

Cody wandered over to get a water bottle. It was getting hot and he was covered in sweat.

"Scoring every game is a bit obnoxious."

Mandy laughed and waved him over.

"Things are going pretty good today. The cross was perfect. I just closed my eyes and let it hit me," Cody said.

"Yeah, right," Mandy said.

Talia joined them.

"I didn't see you guys before. When did you get here?" Cody asked.

"About ten minutes ago," Talia said. "We were down at City Hall for the vote — a bunch of people actually showed up to protest, which was cool. It dragged on and on, though — and we left. We wanted to see a bit of your game. Our moms are still there, of course."

They'd begun to watch each other's games. Cody, Kenneth, Paulo, and Luca had watched Talia and Mandy play the night before.

"How are the moms holding up?" Cody grinned. He could only imagine how crazed Candice would be.

Mandy's answer surprised him. "I talked to my mom

about it last night. She couldn't sleep — too upset. I kinda felt sorry for her. She's made it into a personal thing. The world's not going to end no matter what happens." She yawned and then laughed. "We ended up watching a movie together until three in the morning. I'm exhausted."

"That was nice of you," Cody said to her. "I bet your mom felt better with you there."

Mandy's face turned a bit red. "Not sure about that — but I figured she wanted me to watch with her."

Cody didn't care that he'd said something so personal. Mandy needed to hear that she'd done a good thing — but as Kenneth had taught him, he didn't have to overdo the serious routine, either.

"Feel free to cheer like crazy if we score again — helps the confidence. Name chanting is nice, too," Cody said.

"*Cod-y, Cod-y, he's our man . . .* " Mandy sang in a high-pitched voice.

Cody held up a hand. "Maybe chanting's a bad idea. Let's stick with cheering."

An unfortunately familiar voice began to laugh and clap.

"Can I cheer for you?" Timothy said.

"No," Cody said.

John and Antonio joined Timothy. They were all wearing Storm tracksuits.

Kenneth came over. "You're a bit early for the learn-to-play clinic," Kenneth said. "We can start now, if you want." He pointed to a soccer ball. "That's called a ball. It's round. You kick it with your feet — but no hands allowed."

The rest of the Lions formed a semi-circle around

Kenneth. Michael and Tyler joined their teammates and stood beside Antonio.

"Funny man, as always," Timothy said. "Funny thing is you're not funny. That must be awkward."

"We leave the funny to you. You're a total joke when you play," Luca said.

Timothy looked at them closely, and then he slapped Antonio's shoulder with the back of his hand. "They don't know. Unbelievable. They're as clueless as ever." His mouth twisted into a cruel smile. "The council just got out. They voted. My dad got the call. UPW has the permit. It wasn't even close. I think it was something like fifteen votes to three. Did you guys really think anyone cared what you were doing? For real? How's it feel to waste your summer?"

"They don't know anything," John said. He looked around nervously.

"I didn't ask for your opinion," Cody said. "You want to talk to the Lions — make an appointment." He put his hands on his hips and glared at Timothy.

"Eggy's getting feisty," Timothy said, pretending to pout. "Stick around and see a real team play. You're all giddy 'cause you're beating the Rangers."

"We kicked their butts a week ago," Antonio said.

"Yeah, you won 2–1," Luca said drily.

Cody laughed.

Antonio scowled. "You thinkin' you're tough again?" he said to Cody.

"Sorry," Cody said. "Didn't you get the joke? It was funny because you said you kicked the Rangers' butts, and you barely beat them. We're winning 3–0 at halftime. So . . . it was kinda funny."

His teammates were laughing, and so were Mandy and Talia.

"I guess everyone's a big fat giggle-puss," Timothy sneered. "Maybe we'll see you at City Hall Square tomorrow — the mayor's throwing a welcome party for UPW. I bet Brandon and William will be there — oh, yeah, and Jacob, Ryan, and Austin."

"Sounds great. But do you have to come?" William said.

That did it. The Lions lost it. Timothy tried to make a comeback, but they were laughing too hard to hear him.

"Bunch of goofs," Timothy said.

"We'll see you at the party," Cody said.

Timothy waved at them with the back of his hand and spun away. Cody met John's eyes. Again, as at the lake, he looked very unhappy. He scrunched his mouth to one side, rolled his neck, and slowly walked behind the others.

As suddenly as it had started, the laughter stopped. Reality sunk in quickly — UPW had won.

Mandy looked like she was about to cry. Talia's face had gone white. Paulo's fists were clenched. Kenneth flicked his eyebrows up high, a slight smile on his lips, his head shaking slowly, side-to-side. Luca stared straight ahead, expressionless. Cody didn't know what to feel. He knew one thing, though. The Lions had a game to win.

"This isn't the time, boys," Cody said. "We're in the middle of a battle. We're a team, and UPW doesn't matter right now. Bring it in." He put his hand out. Brandon was the first to put his on top, and then William. Kenneth and

Luca were next, and then everyone else. "This ain't just about the Rangers either," Cody said. "The Storm will be watching every second. We need to send them a message — and that message is you really don't want to play us because we're going to destroy you. Big time. They can talk all they want, but they can't ignore what they see. They're going to see a team that isn't afraid of anyone — or anything."

"On three, boys!" Kenneth shouted.

They counted down and let out a roar.

"Keep the pressure on," David said, as he headed to the net.

"Back line needs to keep aggressive. Force their forwards up the field!" Luca shouted.

"We relax when the score's 8–0," Paulo said.

They all jogged to their positions. Cody went over to Mandy and Talia.

"I'm sorry," he said simply.

"We probably never had a chance," Talia said.

"Waste of time," Mandy muttered. "Timothy was right about one thing."

Cody looked straight at her. "He's wrong. Would you rather we did nothing and just let it happen? How would you feel then? We had forty kids at the lake playing soccer yesterday. We made a great website and Facebook page that hundreds of people visited. We had an online petition with eight hundred and fifty names. And we met a bunch of cool people. A jerk like Timothy isn't going to ruin that for me."

Mandy hunched her shoulders and took a deep breath

— and then smiled. "You're right," she said. "I'm just bummed out. I was hoping for a miracle."

Talia took out her phone and laughed. "That's Mom. She wants me back home. I think I'm going to have a very angry mom on my hands."

Cody expected Mandy to make a joke about her mom.

She surprised him "I should go, too. Mom will be totally upset," she said.

"That's a nice idea," Cody said. He was proud of her. She was putting her family first.

"So I guess you'll be at City Hall tomorrow for the big celebration," Talia said sarcastically.

Cody glanced at the field. The referee was walking toward the circle. He had to get out there. "Absolutely, and both of you will be there, too."

"Don't think so, Cody," Mandy said.

"We're not going to celebrate. We're going to play soccer. The Marathon Game is going on the road. Consider it an away game," Cody said.

The referee blew his whistle.

"We'll talk later," Cody said to the girls. He turned and sprinted back to the field.

The ref put the ball on the spot. The Rangers forward put his foot out.

TWEET!

The forward knocked it to the right, and the ball rolled back to the right midfielder.

"What was that all about?" Paulo said to Cody, as they both pressed forward.

The Rangers midfielder fed it to the right outside back.

"The Marathon Game is on the move," Cody said.

"On the move where?"

"We're going to City Hall tomorrow, bro," Cody said.

"I like the way you're thinkin'," Paulo said.

Cody held his hand down low and they slapped. Cody broke off sharply to help Jordan force the ball to the sideline. Brandon was there to challenge and he stripped it away. He punched it over to Jordan, who one-timed it square to Cody.

He whirled and headed down field. The Lions were on the attack — again.

20

Cody wheeled his bike from the garage, stuffed his ball into his backpack, and set off for City Hall. He turned the corner and heard a voice call out.

CODY, CODY QUITE CONTRARY,

KISSED A GIRL AND MADE HER MERRY.

Kenneth and Luca zoomed up beside him on their bikes.

"Hey, guys. How's the turnout looking?" Cody said.

Mandy had posted the Marathon Game at City Hall as an event on Facebook.

"Not sure — I didn't speak to anyone," Kenneth said. "Doesn't matter. We got the core right here."

"And we've got Señor Paulo, too," Luca said.

Paulo was riding his skateboard on the sidewalk. They slowed down to let him catch up. "You guys know where there's a soccer game?"

"We do, but it's only for awesome players like me," Kenneth said. "You can wipe my sweat off my back with your shirt during breaks if you want?"

"You said I could do that," Luca complained.

Kenneth sighed. "Okay. You can both do it."

"Grab on," Luca said to Paulo. "I'll drag ya."

Paulo hopped the curb and took hold of the back of Luca's bike seat.

They continued on until City Hall came into view. The Square was fairly crowded.

"Is that Ian on stage?" Luca asked.

Cody couldn't see his face, but the yellow Storm hat and his pear-shaped body were a dead giveaway.

"This was a great idea, Cody," Kenneth said. "We get to hear Ian rub it in our face."

This time Cody knew Kenneth was joking. "If the Marathon Game bugs Ian even for a second it'll be worth it," he said.

"You're so right, bro," Kenneth said. "I forgot how much fun it is to irritate Ian."

"If it irritates Timothy, this might be the greatest day of my life," Luca said.

"We might get lucky and irritate John, Antonio, Tyler, and Michael, too," Paulo said.

"You know, I don't think John wants to be with those guys," Cody said. "I feel sorry for him. I could be crazy, but to me it's like he's pretending to be a bully. He's not really like that. I think they give him a seriously hard time. Same with his dad, Mitch."

They locked their bikes up.

"I get the same vibe," Kenneth said. "It's like he's scared all the time. Timothy treats him like garbage, and the rest of the guys follow Timothy, as always."

"Who wouldn't?" Luca said. "Timothy's so follow-able."

Off to the side, Cody noticed a large group of kids — then it hit him. They were all there, all the kids who'd played, including Kyle and his crew, the girls from Mandy and Talia's team, the Fergies, and some kids from Bowmont. His heart swelled with pride. They'd really done something special.

A huge cheer sounded when they came over.

"Don't feel guilty about making us wait," Talia said.

"We wanted to give you a chance to get to know each other," Kenneth said, without skipping a beat. "So what's the score, Mandy?"

"It's actually a tie: 484–484," Mandy said.

"No way," Luca said. "Over three weeks and we're tied?"

"Looks like it," Mandy said.

Talia grinned and slowly pulled Pinky from a bag and held it over her head. Philip and Ashwin dropped to their knees and bowed.

"It still takes my breath away," Luca said.

"Okay, Sad and Pathetic, we've let the McStompers stay close so they won't cry. Now we can put this away and win the hardware," Kenneth said.

"I've kept this a secret long enough. I need to let it out," Luca said. "The Sad and Pathetic Football Club players can't handle pressure. They'll be crying in about five minutes. Pinky is ours."

"We probably have about forty-five people," Isaac said. "It's a big enough space to play eight aside, don't you think?"

"That's ridiculous," Kenneth said. "We only have room to play eight aside."

"You're both idiots," Philip said. "We should play eight aside."

The crackle of the microphone interrupted them.

"Ladies and gentlemen," the mayor said into the microphone. "Thanks for coming, everyone. We're extremely ecstatic to officially welcome UPW into our community. We've worked long and hard to make this happen, and I know I speak on behalf of the entire city council and the entire community when I say we're looking forward to working with you for many years to come. Not to mention the community centre and soccer fields, and the money for the youth sports programs. It's absolutely fantastic — and we're grateful."

He turned to his right with his hands pressed together at his chest, and he bowed his head toward a man wearing a blue, pinstriped suit.

"So, now it gives me enormous pleasure to introduce someone who has become a good friend of mine, and who just happens to be the vice-president of international operations of UPW, Carl Bornsteen."

The man in the suit stepped up to the mic.

"Here comes a shout out for the Marathon Game," Kenneth said, joking.

"I bet he wants Pinky," Cody said.

The kids laughed — to Cody's total relief.

"Thank you for that nice introduction," Bornsteen said. "I like to think I made a lot of new friends — and I know I did and so did UPW. The support we've had from the four city councils in voting to give us a permit to build an ultra-pure water factory at Lake Tawson is really heartwarming. At UPW, we also take great pride in bringing communities together, and obviously this issue has been controversial, even divisive. There have been protests, letters and petitions, websites, even soccer games, all protesting against UPW. We don't necessarily agree that Lake Tawson is at risk, but neither can we give the kind of guarantees the protesters are asking for."

Cody pulled on Mandy's elbow. "This is weird. Something's going on," he said.

"In any event, as you can well imagine, an international company with projects all over the world, often at the same time, cannot be dependent on any single location. We have to keep our options open — a matter of being prudent. So it's unfortunate, but I imagine not too surprising to you," Bornsteen continued, "that UPW has also been pursuing an ultra-pure water factory in India. If you think we have a lot of government regulations here, you should spend some time in that country." He paused, as if waiting for laughter.

The crowd had become completely quiet.

"UPW isn't in the business of making enemies, and I think . . . here . . . we've made some. That combined with UPW receiving permission to build in India two days ago has caused us to change our minds — at least for now. As you can imagine, UPW is terribly disappointed that we won't be here. But at UPW we live by the motto: never say never! And it doesn't change the fact that we're tremendously grateful to everyone who's supported the project and especially to the mayors and the four city councils who granted us a permit. UPW and the entire executive team want you to know we think the world of this place and consider you all to have been fabulous partners. Who knows, maybe we'll be back."

He waved, shook hands with the Mayor, who looked like he needed to sit down, and then Bornsteen left the stage. He walked quickly to a waiting car and sped away. The entire Square had gone eerily quiet. The mayor and Ian looked at each other. Suddenly, Ian threw his hands in the air and starting jabbing his finger into the mayor's chest.

"You said this was in the bag!" Ian shouted, the microphone catching every word.

"It's not my fault ... I didn't know," the mayor stuttered.

Mitch came running over and grabbed the mic. The mayor and Ian continued yelling at each other, toe-to-toe.

"So what just happened?" Mandy said.

"They're not going to build the factory after all?" Cody said.

Suddenly, Cody found himself surrounded by absolute pandemonium. They formed a tight circle and began jumping around, everyone screaming their heads off. No one could use words. It was too much. They'd done it. They'd actually made a difference. UPW had been listening all along.

Talia held Pinky aloft, and some kids started chanting *Pink-y, Pink-y.*

"We gotta regroup at the lake in an hour," Kenneth said when they'd calmed down. "Spread the word. I'll bring the sound system. Lake Tawson deserves a party — a birthday party, for the first day in the rest of her life."

"Give me a Tawson on three," Paulo said.

"One ... two ... three ... "

They threw their hands in the air and screamed.

Luca began to sing:

WE LOVE LAKE TAWSON,

WE THINK SHE'S VERY NICE.

AND IF YOU DON'T AGREE,

YOUR HEAD IS FULL OF LICE.

"I had no idea you were a musical genius," Kenneth gasped.

"Neither did I," Luca said.

They all began to sing it, with Kenneth leading them across the Square. Cody took a look back at the stage. The mayor and Ian were still going at it, with Mitch a couple metres away, holding the mic. The crowd had begun to disperse, with a few dirty looks cast their way. Cody spotted William, Brandon, and the other Lions standing together. Cody went over.

"How insane is this?" Cody said.

"My dad actually knew about it last night, but I was sworn to secrecy," William said. "UPW was freaking out about the protesters, especially the Marathon Game. You guys . . . they're scared of bad publicity because of the problems they've had with other projects. My dad also thinks they were always ready to go to India because it's cheaper. Once things got ugly here they decided to make the move."

"Are your families gonna be okay?" Cody asked.

"UPW had alternative plans, and so did my dad's company," William said.

"My mom told me they have tons of work to do even without UPW, so . . . I guess everything's cool," Brandon said.

Cody thought about his dad. What would Joel do when he heard?

"There may not be a factory on Lake Tawson, but there's going to be a party in about an hour," Cody said. "You guys gotta come. It'll be fun. Kenneth's figuring out the music and . . . you should come."

"Thanks," Brandon said. "It might be kinda weird for us to be there?"

"We weren't part of the Marathon Game," Ryan said. "It's your thing."

"No chance," Cody said. "It's about the lake, not some stupid factory. You have to come — all the Lions gotta be there."

For a moment the five boys looked at him.

"If the Lions are going — we'll be there," William said.

"Awesome," Cody said. He looked over his shoulder.

The Marathon Gamers were marching down the street. Kenneth and Luca were unlocking their bikes. "Lake Tawson in one hour," he ordered.

"No problem."

"See ya, Cody."

"Take it easy.

He barely felt the ground under his feet as he ran over to his bike. The Lions were a team again — united — and he'd made a ton of new friends and Lake Tawson was going to be okay. And if UPW came back, so would the Marathon Game.

He was worried about his dad, even though William and Brandon's parents were okay. He unlocked his bike and set off for his house.

21

The front door was wide open. Something bad must have happened! Cody's heart sped as he raced up the stairs and into his house.

"Hey, Cody. Is that you?" his mom called out cheerfully from the living room.

"Yeah." He hesitated. "How are you guys?"

"We're fine," his dad said. "Don't be shy. Come on in."

His dad didn't sound like himself, and he had a goofy expression on his face.

"How'd it go?" his mom asked.

"You don't know?"

"We've been here most of the morning," his dad said.

"What did you get to eat this time?" his mom asked.

"They didn't have food," Cody began.

"Typical," his mom said. "They spend like mad until

they get the permit, and then the wallet closes tight. I bet they never build the community centre. You can quote me on that."

"You win that bet," Cody said.

His dad gave him a puzzled look. "How come you're so sure?"

"How come you're not at work?" Cody replied.

His mom and dad smiled at each other.

"I am at work," he said.

"You're working at home now, like Mom?"

"No — I'm getting an office," his dad grinned.

"Oh, stop it, Sean," his mom said. "Your father is teasing you, Cody."

"I quit my job," his dad said. "I didn't want to tell you until everything was settled."

"But . . . why?"

"Let's say I was inspired by a young boy who believed in himself, a young boy who wasn't going to give in — and who had the courage to be there for his family. I've been complaining about my job for too long. I've been afraid of Joel for way too long. I've been cheating you guys by not being the person I want to be. To make a long story short, two other friends and I are starting our own company. We were asked to take on a big contract and it was too good an opportunity to pass up. I've been thinking about it for years — and now we're doing it."

Cody began laughing. It was too much.

"I'm glad you find my business plans so amusing," his dad said.

"It's not that," Cody said. "It's that . . . It's . . . I don't know how to say it. It still sounds impossible. At the celebration today, down at City Hall Square, the mayor introduced this UPW guy, Bornsteen, and he announced that UPW wasn't going to build a factory on Lake Tawson after all. They decided to build in India instead."

His parents stared at him in disbelief.

"I'm serious," Cody said. "He thanked everyone for the support, got in a car, and drove off."

His dad sat back in his chair and ran his hand across his forehead. "That's the most amazing thing I've ever heard." A sad look crossed his face. "Some of the people at my office are going to lose their jobs."

"Maybe someone can hire them?" his mom said.

His dad flicked his eyebrows. "Maybe that's a good idea."

"A few of the guys are meeting down at the lake — kinda like a celebration. Is it okay if I go?" Cody said.

"Who's going, exactly?" his mom said.

"The people who played in the Marathon Game."

"Will Mandy be there?" his mom asked.

"I guess — and Talia. She's her friend."

The doorbell rang.

"Is that for you?" his mom said.

Cody walked into the hallway. Kenneth's face peered back through the front door window, and he saw Paulo and Luca behind him.

"I think the guys are here," he said.

"Just the guys?" His mom grinned and raised her eyebrows.

Cody laughed. He needed to lighten up about girls. He liked Mandy. So what? They had something special in common.

He stepped back into the kitchen. "Glad to hear you're doing what you want, Dad," he said. "I'm . . . proud of you, too."

"Thanks, Cody."

"You have an early practice tomorrow, so not too late," his mom said.

"Okay."

He went to the front door.

"Where is everyone?" Cody asked.

"We just zipped home to tell the parental units where we were going," Kenneth said.

Cody had to laugh at himself. He'd been so uptight about leaving the others as they left City Hall Square — and Kenneth just admitted it straight out.

"Let's make tracks," Luca said. "The girls need us — they'll be all scared by themselves."

"Not sure Mandy's scared of much," Paulo said.

Cody knew her better than that. He knew the scrappy, tough, talented soccer player was also sad, in pain, worried, and lonely. She was, he hoped, his very good friend.

"Repeat after me, everyone," Kenneth said. "*UPW is really dumb.*"

The boys repeated the line, military style.

"*Ian's a jerk and his son's a bum . . .*"

The ride over felt like it took two seconds. They locked their bikes and raced down the path. Cody charged up the sand dune right behind Kenneth.

"Whoa, boys," Kenneth said, throwing his arms out.

Cody skidded to a stop.

"Traffic on this beach is a killer," Cody said.

Kenneth gave him a look. "You keep this up and you're going to develop a sense of humour," he said.

"I doubt it," Cody said.

Truth was he was feeling strangely silly, as if he might break out laughing any second. He'd been fighting the urge ever since they left his house.

"Not sure I expected this," Luca said, coming up beside Cody.

At least a hundred kids were dancing by the water, with two speakers belting out the tunes. Kenneth pulled a little speaker out of his backpack. "I'm feeling kinda inadequate right about now," he said.

"Paulo, did you call dial-a-party?" Luca asked.

Paulo seemed too surprised to answer. Cody spotted the Fergies dancing away in the lake. Kyle and his buds were dancing with some girls from Mandy and Talia's team.

"It's like a commercial for a soft drink," Cody said.

"If there's gonna be a commercial, we gotta be the stars," Kenneth said. "Luca — initiate awesome dance moves."

"Way ahead of ya, bro," Luca said. He stiffened up, bent his arms ninety degrees, and began to walk jerkily down the sand dune.

"You ain't seriously going with the robot?" Kenneth said.

"People love it," Luca said, over his shoulder.

"Maybe fifty years ago," Paulo said.

Luca stopped and turned around slowly, keeping his body rigid. "Think how stupid you'd feel if we get caught in a time warp and get transported back in time, and everyone sees you doing fancy hip hop moves and I'm totally fitting in with the robot. They'll throw you in jail for being freaks, and I'll be the coolest guy here."

"I hate to admit it: the dude's totally right," Kenneth said.

"The robot it is," Paulo said.

Paulo began dancing down the sand dune, robot-style. Kenneth slapped hands with Cody and followed, arms bent, twisting jerkily at the waist, feet shuffling. Cody's good mood vanished. He basically never danced in public. He was *that kid*, the one who sat on the gym bleachers and counted down the minutes before his mom came and picked him up. He could never shake the feeling that everyone was watching him and thinking he looked like a loser.

The girls from Mandy and Talia's team spotted them first and began cheering. Then the Fergies joined in and began clapping to the beat. Cody could feel the sweat break out on the back of his neck. Everyone was watching — everyone.

Cody took a jerky step forward and bent his arms.

Better to look like a loser, than be a loser.

He shuffled down the dune quickly to catch up.

"Kickin' it old-school!" Philip cried out. "I love it."

Ashwin began doing the robot, too — more like a robot on steroids — and that decided things. All the kids joined in, and then slowly, without anyone organizing it, they formed a huddle and began bouncing in the air in rhythm, hooting and hollering, screaming and yelling.

For the next ten minutes, Cody and his buds high-fived and hugged and slapped hands with practically everyone.

People were lining up to congratulate them and to thank them for saving the lake. Cody got tired of saying everyone should get the credit. Someone tapped him on the shoulder and he turned, expecting another round of hugs and high-fives.

Mandy smiled and she hopped up on her toes.

A song started up and she shook her hips a couple of times, and with a shy grin said, "I've seen you. Don't pretend you can't dance."

"I don't pretend — I really can't," Cody said.

"I'll teach you," she said quietly. She took his hand and swung it gently left and then right.

"Am I supposed to do something?"

"Spin, dummy."

"Right. Gotcha."

He did his best imitation of a spin, and almost fell.

"Watch. Bend your knee a bit, and keep your centre of gravity over your foot." She spun three times — and then bowed gracefully. "Six years of ballet," she explained.

This girl was incredible — ballerina and hard-nosed midfielder. Quite a combo.

Mandy took a step forward, her eyes cast down slightly. "Seems like a dream, like this can't be real," she said.

"Don't get mad if I say this," he said. "Only for me . . . it's like this is what's real, and the other parts of my life, like when I was sick and in treatment, and even after it, when I started playing soccer again, that wasn't real. I wasn't myself, too worried about everything, about what people thought of me, embarrassed about the cancer . . . "

"You're right," Mandy said. "I spend too much time

upset about Gavin and being angry at my mom for pretending everything's all right and for getting obsessed with things, like blaming UPW for Gavin — and for crying herself to sleep every night when she thinks I can't hear."

"Have you ever thought," Cody said, "that maybe . . . and I'm not saying I know . . . but maybe you're mad at your mom because she won't let you forget about Gavin? Maybe . . . sometimes . . . you don't want to remember?"

They were surrounded by kids, all dancing on the beach, laughing and having a good time. Yet he felt as if he was alone with Mandy, inside a bubble, inside their own little world.

"Gavin would've liked this," Mandy said, staring out onto the lake.

"I obviously didn't know Gavin," Cody said, "but I bet if he could talk to you he'd say: 'Have a great time, Mandy — but remember me once in a while and it's okay to be sad for me'."

A tear fell down her cheek.

A new song came on, this one with a slow beat. Kids began dancing in pairs or in a group, arms around each other's shoulders. Mandy put her arms around Cody's neck. They were so light he barely felt them.

"I know it's dumb," she said, "but I couldn't stop thinking that this was my last chance, that if UPW won the vote I'd never be happy again, as if UPW was this dark cloud hanging over me. Now that UPW's gone . . . " She was struggling with her words. "Nothing's really changed. My mom is still — Mom. Gavin is still . . . gone. And I still don't know how to deal with all that."

"What's changed is now you know the problem," Cody said. "Trust me. That makes a huge difference. Sounds dumb, but I think I forgot how to have fun and be a kid. I was like this ultra-serious eighty-year-old man. Once I figured that out, things felt different, and not because UPW's going to India and now life is perfect. I decided that I'm not going to be Cody, the kid who had cancer. I'm just going to be Cody — and if you don't like that, too bad."

"I like this Cody," Mandy said.

Cody felt himself blush.

The music began to speed up. Mandy took her arms away from Cody's neck and began to dance. He took her hand and spun her around three times. Cody caught Kenneth's eye. He was dancing with Talia. He stuck out his tongue. Luca danced past Cody and gave him a gentle elbow in the back.

"We've got a practice tomorrow," Luca said. "Don't get tired."

Paulo lifted his chin and nodded to Cody, his eyes half-closed. Paulo danced like he played soccer: cool, smooth, and in control. A few girls were in a semi-circle in front of him.

Cody heard a few kids cheering. Kenneth had put Talia on his shoulders and they were careening around, Talia shrieking, Kenneth barely managing to keep his feet.

"Up you get," Cody said to Mandy.

He bent down and she hopped on his shoulders. Kenneth spotted them and barrelled over. Mandy and Talia joined hands and the boys danced away, surrounded by the joyful crowd, music blasting a steady beat, sun shining, and the waves lapping softly on the warm sand.

WANT TO FIND OUT HOW CODY GOT HIS START ON THE LIONS?

Read the Silver Birch Finalist *Striker* for the exciting story of what happened before Cody and his friends came together for *The Beautiful Game*.

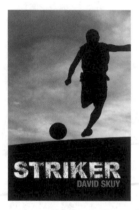

It's been almost a year since thirteen-year-old Cody was diagnosed with cancer for a tumour in his leg. Now he's ready to start playing soccer again, if he can convince his mom to let him try out. Though it's a struggle, Cody makes the team as a sub. But things aren't right on the Lions, and after a team shake-up, he finds himself with more playing time than he thinks he can handle. Can Cody find the strength and the courage to get his A-game back?

PRAISE FOR STRIKER:

"This engaging sports story will keep readers entertained and thinking."
— *VOYA Top Shelf Middle Grade*

"*Striker* is a fast paced novel about soccer that touches on sensitive issues such as cancer, bullying and racism. . . A fun novel for reluctant readers. Recommended."
— *CM: Canadian Review of Materials*

"*Striker* is a thoroughly enjoyable, sporty novel . . . with strong messages about friendship, teamwork, and overcoming obstacles."
— *Resource Links*

"Skuy adeptly combines exhilarating sports with a thoughtfully engrossing storyline that will inspire readers."
— *Kirkus Reviews*